RIKA CORONATED

THE GENEVIAN QUEEN – BOOK 2

BY M. D. COOPER

Thanks to the Aeon 14
Just in Time (JIT) & Beta Readers

Timothy Van Oosterwyk Bruyn
Gareth Banks
Chad Burroughs
Gene Bryan
Scott Reid
Steven Blevins
David Wilson

Version 1.0.0

ISBN: 978-1-64365-039-5

Cover Art by Tek Tan
Editing by Jen McDonnell, Bird's Eye Books

TABLE OF CONTENTS

FOREWORD

Nothing like finishing a novel in the nick of time! As I'm writing this, there are still a few scenes to review, but other than the edits, Rika Coronated is in the can!

That's good, because I'm sitting on a plane headed for Orlando, and Disney World. Last year, I'd missed the 'Disney deadline' and was working on *Impact Imminent* in the evenings after rides and walking all day. This year, I was determined to put the deadline stress out of my mind and enjoy myself with more time for family fun.

At the end of the week, we're off to Cape Canaveral for a book signing and a tour of the Kennedy Space Center. A good number of readers will be there, and I'm looking forward to some great conversations and a few games of Snark.

It's funny how our yearly pilgrimages to Florida and Disney always coincide with author events. It's a bit of a chicken or the egg question as to which came first. We may never know....

Be that as it may, I'm looking forward to some relaxation before the final few days of going through edits and final refinements before this book releases. I find that the extra recharge gets me excited for the final stretch of the novel's prep as well as sharing it with you in my newsletter and social media.

I have a few other projects going on this summer; one of which is a kitchen remodel, and the others are a new series following a not-so-gentlemanly gentleman named Jax

Bremen. That story will not be officially branded as Aeon 14 due to some publishing restrictions, but don't worry, it's really an Aeon 14 story and takes place during the Dark Ages which followed the FTL wars. Plus, there's *Decisive Action*, *The Spreading Fire*, the Sera and Jessica book...the list goes on.

I'm also working on a tabletop pen and paper RPG (role-playing game) set in Aeon 14. This project came about after the owner of a popular RPG company read Destiny Lost and realized that Aeon 14 would make an amazing universe to set a game in.

The plan is for the first adventure to take place during the events of Aeon 14, following a group that is sent to secure tech in and around the Bollam's World System during the months when Tanis is missing.

If it does well, you can count on there being a Marauders Expansion!

There are a few more stories to tell about Rika and her Genevian Marauders before the Orion War wraps up. I plan to have one more out before book 12 of The Orion War (*Return to Sol*), and then we'll see where Rika's adventures take her next.

M. D. Cooper
Danvers 2019

THE JOURNEY THUS FAR

The Marauders were always meant to liberate Genevia.

When General Mill formed the mercenary company at the end of the first war with Nietzschea, he thought it would be the work of a lifetime to save his former nation. He had not anticipated the effect of Rika and her mechs, nor the near-miraculous tech that the ISF brought to the table.

Once, the Genevian mechs were just a level or two above horror-show freaks. Human and machine grafted together with the only goal being to make them more efficient killing machines.

The mechs' encounter with Tangel and the ISF changed that, making their cyborg bodies truly feel like one being, streamlining and optimizing them in every way. Though they look more human—should they choose—the Genevian mechs are far more deadly than they have ever been before.

Add to that the advanced nanotech that Tangel granted to several mechs in leadership positions—the stasis shields for their ships, and CriEn power modules to run them—and the Marauders have become as fierce a fighting force as the ISF Marines.

Tangel and the ISF effectively hired the Marauder mercenary organization to defeat the Nietzscheans and take back Genevia, but Tangel only did it to give what Rika was going to do anyway a veil of legitimacy. Intel that Chase gathered in the Parsons System led the Marauders to learn that Emperor Constantine, leader of the Nietzschean Empire, was in the

Genevia System—former capital of the Genevian Alliance—overseeing the final stages of an invasion fleet's construction.

Rika and her mechs killed the Nietzschean emperor and, with the assistance of an ISF fleet, took control of the Genevia System.

With that victory, Rika realized that she could not continue her lightning attack, driving through Old Genevia like a spear aimed at the heart of her enemy's empire. The people of Genevia needed clear leadership, and what's more, the Niets had begun a scorched-earth withdrawal from other systems, requiring the mechs to provide aid and plan for the defense of their people.

Rika also suspects that the Niets will use this tactic to weaken her position in the Genevia System so they can mount a counterattack.

This is exacerbated by conflict with elements within the former resistance forces who do not wish to share power with the mechs, as well as Nietzschean agents who still have their hooks deep in the Genevians.

Attacks on Rika's life, and ultimately the theft of the *Pinnacle,* an advanced super-dreadnought with the ability to fire through stasis shields, brought us to the culmination of the prior book's adventure.

We left Rika and her Marauders in orbit of Babylon, a gas giant in the Genevia System, where her mechs secured the *Pinnacle,* but not before it destroyed her flagship, the *Fury Lance.*

PROMINENT CHARACTERS

Though there is a full list of all the mechs, pilots, and members of the Marauders at the end of the book, this is a listing of some of the more prominent characters and their current role in the battalion.

Genevian Marauders Leadership

Rika – Magnus, commander in chief of the Genevian Marauders
Silva – Colonel, commander of the Queen's Guard
Barne – Major General, commander of the Marauders' First Division
Leslie – Colonel, head of the GM Military Intelligence
Niki – AI, Captain, operations officer

1st Marauder Battalion

Chase – Colonel, battalion commanding officer
Penelope – Lieutenant Colonel, executive officer

Other Key Characters

Tremon – Former Genevian President (known as Kalvin)
Arla – Former Genevian Minister of Finance, attempted to take control of the mechs
Carson – ISF (Intrepid Space Force) Admiral

The Seventh Fleet, First Division

Heather (Smalls) – Captain of the *Fury Lance*

Travis – Captain of the *Republic*
Ferris – Lieutenant, commander of the *Undaunted*
Vargo Klen – Lieutenant, commander of the *Asora*
Ashley – CWO, bridge crew aboard the *Asora*
Buggsie – Lieutenant, commander of the *Capital*

MAPS

For more maps, and full-size versions, visit www.aeon14.com/maps.

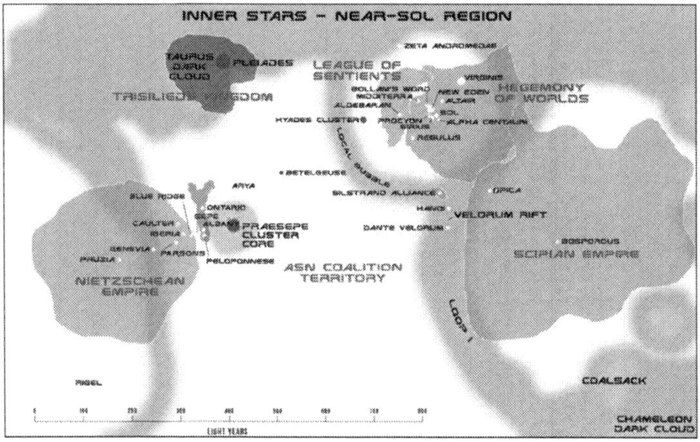

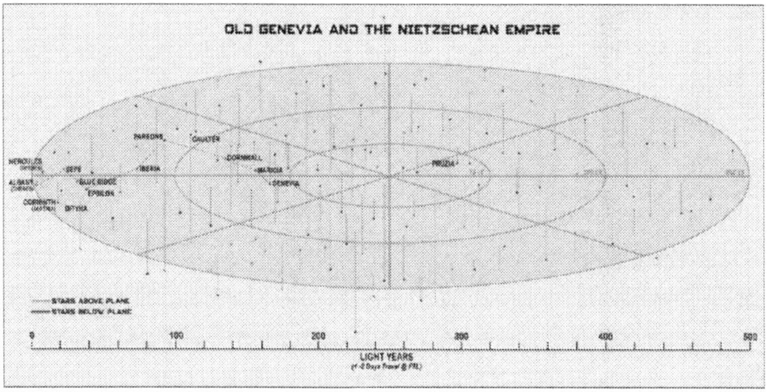

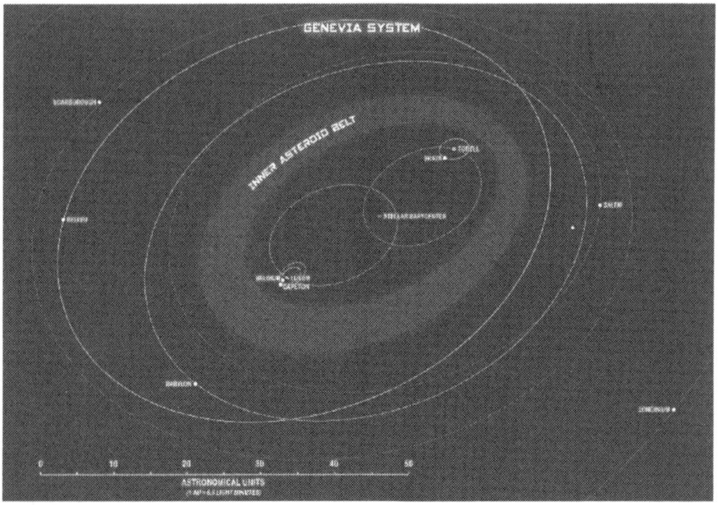
GENEVIA SYSTEM
INNER ASTEROID BELT
0
10
20
30
40
50
ASTRONOMICAL UNITS

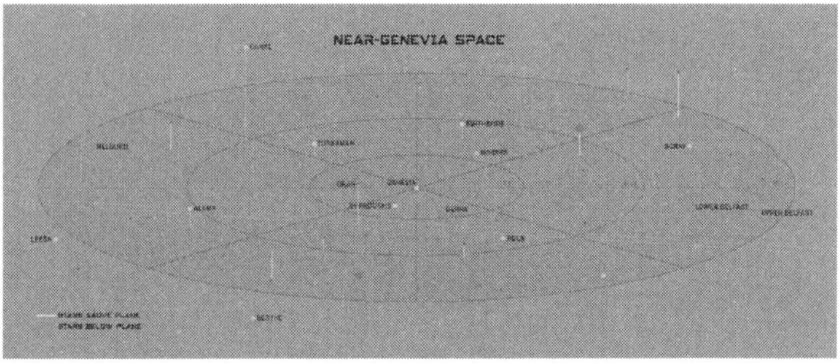
NEAR-GENEVIA SPACE

A LITTLE HEIST

STELLAR DATE: 06.03.8950 (Adjusted Years)
LOCATION: Corinth City, Chad
REGION: Burroughs System, Old Genevia, Nietzschean Empire

Rajiz glanced at Avi and shook his head.

"Seriously? We're going to break into a Nietzschean compound with you wearing that?"

Avi looked down at her sparkling blue, painted-on skinsuit. "Why not? The Niets all love it when I get a bit of glitter on them. They're normally so dour."

"Because this is a *stealth* mission." He bit back a groan and put a hand on her shoulder. "I know your MO is to bang everything that moves as a distraction, but the bastards are twitchy right now. I have a plan that will work a lot better."

She fixed Rajiz with a cold stare, cocking a hip and one eyebrow. "My bang method *always* works, twitchy Niets or not. Why are you doubting me now?"

"General chatter I've picked up. Something's bothering their commanders." He nodded to the duffle on the ground between them. "There's a spare coverall in there. Just put it on."

Avi grunted. "The biggest crimes we'll be committing today are against fashion. Is it at least fitted? I'm not going to wear a potato sack, like you have on," she muttered while bending to slide open the duffle's fastener.

"Yeah. I know you that well, at least. It has EM-dampening, too."

Avi brushed a hand against her thigh. "This has EM-dampening as well. As in it dampens the electrical signals in Nietzschean brains when they look at my bod."

"Just put it on."

"Fine. You're no fun, you know that, right?"

"I'm the captain, I'm not supposed to be fun."

The platinum-haired woman pouted at him for a moment. "Such a waste."

"This trip to Chad's gonna be a waste if you don't get ready," he whispered angrily. "The Niets're packing a lot of stuff up, moving it somewhere. That's the best time to make a little grab without anyone being the wiser."

Avi muttered something under her breath as she pulled out a matte black shipsuit with a repair company's logo on the chest. Smoothing the fabric across her hips, she sighed.

"More like 'not disgustingly baggy', not fitted."

"Stars, woman. Are you going to be ready sometime today?"

While his first mate uttered a fresh round of curses under her breath, Rajiz went back to looking over the Nietzschean compound through the blinds of the office building they'd snuck into.

Though the Niets had been on Chad since the end of the war, they didn't have much use for the single inner planet. The Burroughs System's wealth lay in its two unique ice-giants, both of which produced a unique ammonia-laced diamond in their upper atmosphere.

Aside from having a host of applications in technology and medicine, the diamonds were en vogue with the Nietzschean elite as a fashion accessory.

Chad had gained a bit of popularity as a resort planet amongst the upper management of the mining interests that worked around the ice-giants, but otherwise existed as little more than a convenient, already established food production world.

Despite Chad's general lack of importance, the role it played in supporting outer system mining operations meant that the Niets maintained a few garrisons on the surface. Luckily, they weren't the best troops the occupiers had to offer, and their supplies and gear were easy pickings for Rajiz and the crew of the *ViperTalon*.

"OK, you happy?" Avi said as she pulled up the shipsuit's fastener.

He glanced at her, and gave a reluctant nod. "Yeah. Now focus on the mission, we need to get that case. In, out, on our way. No hanky-panky. I know how much you like to beard the lion in his den."

"I prefer lions without beards," Avi replied with a wink.

Rajiz ignored her and reached out to the *Talon*'s engineer over the team's channel.

<Gero, you ready?>

<Yeah, sure. Betty's in position as well. Whenever you get

your ass in gear, I'll be on my mark.>

<*Don't give me that shit, Gero. I know you're cortex-deep in a sim. Shut it down and get your mind on the task at hand.*>

<*I can multitask,*> Gero protested.

<*Sure,*> Avi joined in. <*Like that time you nearly multitasked us into jail in the Parsons System?*>

<*That was different.*>

<*I don't care.*> Rajiz kept his tone calm, but let a hint of malice flow into the words. <*Get out of the sim, and do your job. Or I'll find someone else who can, and leave you here on Chad.*>

<*Sheesh, Boss. I'm out, I'm out. I have the drone feeds up on all my holos. Things are busy inside the compound, but the patrols haven't changed. Still just two at the gate and two in each tower on the corners.*>

<*And the back gate?*> Rajiz pressed.

<*Unguarded, but locked up tight.*>

<*Good, that's still our way in, then.*>

Avi shouldered the duffle. <*Care to share* ***how*** *we'll get in through a locked gate?*>

<*Nope!*> Rajiz grinned at his first mate. <*You'll just have to wait and see. But it's genius. Trust me.*>

He led the way out of the office building and across the street to a row of low warehouses that fronted the southern approach to the Nietzschean compound.

A patrol moved through the deepening dusk a hundred meters further down the street, but Rajiz ignored them. Given that the pair were on the western end of Corinth City's spaceport, the area was far from deserted, with groundcars, haulers, and smatterings of pedestrians visible in every direction. Two more civilians weren't going to register on the Niets' radar.

An open-topped groundcar waited for them, and Rajiz hopped in, taking the manual controls while Avi settled in beside him. He pulled away from the curb and threaded the maze of warehouses before reaching a road that led around the compound's perimeter to the closed gate.

<*Isn't this a bit suspicious?*> Avi asked, giving him a sidelong look. <*Driving to the closed gate?*>

<*Look at the logo on your suit.*> Rajiz kept his eyes on the road. <*We work for a company that operates out of a hangar just past the compound. This road is almost a direct route there.*>

<*Oh...look at that. It's like you're smart or something.*>

He snorted at her statement. <*Yeah, almost like I've done this before.*>

<*Hey, I've done it with you pretty much every time.*>

A snort came from Gero. <*That's what she said.*>

<*Stars,*> Avi muttered. <*Are you ever going to grow up, Gero?*>

<*Fuck no. Don't say hurtful things like that.*>

<*Keep a lid on it,*> Rajiz grunted as he triggered a failure on the groundcar right in front of the turnoff to the gate.

He swore aloud and leapt out of the car, kicking a wheel before pulling open the battery panel.

"Hunk of junk," he muttered. "Thing never makes it as far as it should on a full charge."

"Need a hand?" Avi asked. "I could get out and push."

"Funny. No, it died in drive, so unless you think you can push a wormgear, it's not moving."

<*OK, so we're stuck in front of a gate no one uses. How—*>

Just as Avi began to complain, the compound gate opened, and a truck drove into view.

<*See? You should just trust me,*> Rajiz said.

<*Or you could say, 'they bring the trash truck out through this gate'.*>

<*And miss seeing you get all flustered over nothing? It's the simple things, you know.*>

Stone barricades lined the short road between the stalled groundcar and the gate, giving the garbage truck nowhere to go. The hauler stopped, and the driver climbed out of the vehicle, storming toward Rajiz.

"What the ever-loving fuck, buddy? Move that piece of crap!"

"Sorry." Rajiz shrugged. "I can't seem to get it to start up. We're gonna need to call for a tow."

<*How is this less conspicuous than me just banging a few people?*> Avi asked.

<*Because you're **memorable**. I should know.*>

"And you're a ship maintenance company?" the truck driver muttered. "Remind me never to fly in something that one of your crews worked on."

"Tow's going to be here in twenty," Rajiz said,

dismissing the driver's remark. "Then we'll be out of your way."

"Twenty! I have a schedule to keep, you idiot."

Rajiz lifted his hands and shrugged. "Hey, getting angry at me isn't going to make it go faster. I don't work on groundcars. Why don't you go through the front entrance?"

The other man shook his head. "No can do. Stuff's all over the place over there, and they won't let me through that gate. They—"

"What in the core is going on here?" another voice broke in.

Rajiz turned to see a Nietzschean with corporal's insignia stride through the gate, giving the garbage truck a sidelong look of disgust as she passed by.

"This fucknut is blocking the road," the truck driver jerked a thumb in Rajiz's direction.

"Not on purpose," Rajiz protested. "I have a tow coming, it'll be here in—"

"Twenty minutes!" The garbage truck driver was reddening visibly.

"Can't you push it?" the corporal asked.

"You can sure try," Rajiz laughed. "Probably easier to lift it, though. You have a loader in there that can do it?"

"Loaders are busy," the corporal shook her head. "But I can grab a squad. Nietzschean muscle can lift your piece of crap."

"Corporal!" A private jogged past the garbage truck. "LT says he wants the gate shut."

The woman looked at the short stretch between the gate and the road and the garbage truck, blowing out a long breath, knowing there wasn't room for the truck to pull out of the compound. "OK, buddy, back it up. We'll have to wait inside till their hauler is towed."

The man grunted something unintelligible and slouched back to his truck.

The corporal stared at Rajiz and Avi for a minute before she jerked a thumb over her shoulder. "You two, inside. It's against policy to allow anyone to loiter outside the gate."

<But we can loiter inside?> Avi commented with a laugh. *<I love stupid policies.>*

<When we get in, look for the first chance to slip away. Gero, has our prize moved at all?>

<Not that I can see,> the engineer replied. *<It's not scheduled to go anywhere anytime soon. Wow, almost everything else is getting packed up, though.>*

Rajiz nodded as he walked into the compound, noting that there was activity everywhere—and not the normal kind. Niets were scurrying about like ants whose hill had been kicked.

"Busy day," he said to the corporal, keeping the woman's attention on him as Avi walked around the garbage truck, disappearing between the rows of equipment stacked next to the gate.

"Could say that," the corporal muttered. "Lot going on."

"Really?" Rajiz asked, wondering if the activity in the

compound had anything to do with the rumors coming out of the Genevia System—rumors of a significant Nietzschean defeat. “You all going on an exercise?”

“You could say that.”

“Where to?” The garbage truck driver leant out his window and stared down at the pair.

“Nonayourbusinesswhere,” the corporal shot back. “Look, just stay where you are while—”

“Wait a second.” Rajiz nodded toward a hauler a hundred meters away. “Is that thing loaded with Razers?”

“What's a Razer?” the driver asked.

“No,” the corporal blurted. “Just standard loadout surveillance drones.”

Rajiz passed his optical feed back to Gero. *<Big G, what do you see here?>*

<Nietzscheans. So many Nietzscheans.>

<On the hauler, you idiot.>

<Oh, those are Razers. I remember because they hit New Mars with them back at the end of the war. Sucked balls. So many balls. All the ba—>

<I get the picture. Did we know they had those things on Chad?>

There was a brief pause, then the engineer gave a noncommittal grunt. *<Not in the inventories I have, but we didn't get the compound's full list.>*

<Sure, yeah, we didn't get shit like toiletries, but the data we got should have had Razers on it.>

<Oh, hell, look at the stamp on the wings.>

<*Where?*> Rajiz asked.

<*Near the tips, where they're folded back.*>

The *ViperTalon*'s captain eyed the arrowhead-shaped drones and spotted what Gero had pointed out. <*OK…that's the 1171*st *Nietzschean fleet's logo.*>

<*Yeah, and those 1171*st *frigates just arrived insystem two days ago.*>

Rajiz ran a hand through his hair, glad that the garbage truck driver was keeping the corporal engaged in small talk.

<*They're bringing Razers downworld? Why?*> he asked, knowing that there weren't many answers, and none of the ones he could think of were good.

<*Bad stuff, Captain. I just keep the engines lit, I don't know why they'd use those things on Chad—oh shit…maybe I do.*>

<*Spill it,*> the captain said, resisting the urge to ask Avi what was taking so long.

<*Feeds just lit up with messages about a Niet merchant convoy that just jumped in from Genevia.*>

<*And?*> Rajiz didn't want to start flipping through public feeds while inside the compound. His conversation with Gero was already risky enough.

<*Genevia's been completely taken by some merc outfit called the Marauders.*>

<*The whosawhat?*>

<*Beats me,*> Gero snorted. <*But they've got quite the fleet, if these chuckleheads are telling the—oh double nut shit. The emperor's dead.*>

<*The Nietzschean emperor?*>

<No, Boss, my toolbox's emperor. Yes, the Nietzschean emperor.>

The *ViperTalon*'s captain looked over the bustling compound, noting that a group of techs were pulling Razers off the hauler, and moving them to a staging area were several of the drones were being configured for flight.

<Avi, get your ass back here. We're leaving the moment the tow arrives.>

<I'm on my way back, I found it.>

<Good. We're making a beeline to the ship. Time to leave Chad in our engine wash. Gero, get the tow here five minutes ago.>

<About this thing I've grabbed,> Avi said. *<The case is almost as big as I am, I don't know that I can hide it.>*

Rajiz chuckled. *<Toss it in the truck.>*

<What?> Avi made a short choking sound. *<The case is Linked. I thought you were going to shut that off before we go? It's going to trigger an alarm as soon as it passes through the gate.>*

<Sure.> He shot her a grin. *<Except that the truck is shielded. The driver and our friend the corporal already have a bit of a grift going on. We're just leveraging their op.>*

<Another detail that would have been nice to know,> Avi muttered as she appeared at the back of the truck. "Shit, that smells like…shit."

"Where were you?" the corporal asked.

"Trying to get upwind," she retorted. "No chance of that, though."

"Oh, tow's here early," Rajiz interrupted, a broad smile on his lips. "If you open the gate up, we'll get out of your hair."

The Nietzschean's eyes darted to the side, and then she nodded. "OK, yeah, let's get this show on the road."

Five minutes later, Rajiz and Avi were sitting in the back of the tow truck, keeping an eye on the garbage hauler that was following them down the road.

<*So, we going to get the case?*> she asked. <*I don't fancy sticking around if this planet's gonna get thrashed by Razers.*>

Rajiz sucked in a slow, deep breath. <*Yeah, we'll get it. The Niets aren't going to make their move for a few more days. We'll know when time's running out.*>

<*How so?*>

<*The Niets are pulling off Chad.*> Rajiz couldn't help the worry in his mental tone. <*Gero picked up a group of troop transports heading insystem. Bastards won't make their move till their people get off-world. Once those transports start settling down, then the clock starts ticking.*>

Avi pursed her lips and her gaze swept across Corinth City. <*Rajiz…we have to do something.*>

<*We are. We're gonna finish our heist and then run. I'm done with war.*>

A TERRIBLE VIEW

STELLAR DATE: 06.03.8950 (Adjusted Years)
LOCATION: Mount Genevia, Belgium
REGION: Genevia System, New Genevian Alliance

Tremon's eyes grew wide as the visuals coming from Babylon showed a beam burst through the planet's cloudtops and strike the *Fury Lance.*

"Shit…." He whispered the word and pursed his lips.

The mechs' attack craft had already left the ship, but he had no way of knowing if Rika was on the *Lance,* or if she'd dropped with her company.

A hand settled on his shoulder, and he glanced in surprise at Detective Kora, having forgotten she was present.

"Don't worry. There's no way Rika was on that thing," she said. "You know she wouldn't stay behind."

He closed his eyes and nodded before replying, "You're right. But still…Heather, Bondo, and half a dozen other Marauders I count as family will have been aboard."

"It's breaking up slowly." Kora activated a holo on the balcony where the pair stood. "They might get off."

The former president nodded, and then the realization hit that the title granted him by Rika placed him at the top of the civilian government if she was dead.

Shit. Not again.

<Admiral Vargo,> he called up to the *Asora*. *<We need to get search and rescue out there. Do we have ships that can go through the clouds?>*

*<**Captain** Vargo,>* the man corrected. *<Legally, Admiral Mior and I are different people. And honestly, I prefer to be Vargo.>*

<Uh, sure…sorry. But about Rika—>

<Don't worry, Chancellor. We already have two stasis destroyers en route. They'll be there within fourteen hours. Plus, High Garden Station is also preparing to send their S&R ships. >

Tremon gave a slow nod, transmitting his resigned acknowledgment over the Link. *<Keep me posted.>*

<Of course, sir.>

<Don't call me 'sir',> he replied, trying to add levity to the somber mood. *<Or I'll call you governor **and** admiral.>*

<Deal.>

"Two destroyers are on their way," Tremon said to Kora, who was staring at him intently. "We'll have to hope for the best."

"No hope necessary," Kora replied. "I've soaked up every bit of vid there is on Queen Rika. She'll come out swinging. No way she won't."

A wary smile settled on Tremon's lips. "Well, history is on your side. Not many people out there have weathered what she has."

"And come out smiling." Kora gave Tremon one of her own, though it was sharper and toothier than his.

"I know you were to report on Oda and Arla's network," he said, returning them to their original reason for meeting, "but I have a thousand people burning up my Link right now. Stars, I need a press secretary."

"Don't even *think* of me for that," she replied. "I'd probably be up for murder charges in a week."

"Take you that long?" Tremon cocked an eyebrow.

"Funny. OK, I can give you the abbreviated version and then get out of your hair."

He nodded for her to continue, dismissing the holodisplay that showed the spreading wreckage of the *Fury Lance*.

"So far as I can tell, Oda really did spend the past decade or so tucked away inside of the Refuge. Arla, however, has been flitting about a few different systems, establishing a resistance called the PLI."

"Seriously? She was doing something altruistic?"

Kora shrugged. "Maybe less altruistic, and more like she just couldn't let power go and had to be in charge of something. Word is that she wasn't exactly the nicest resistance leader. Though she *was* effective."

"This doesn't surprise me. Rika's right, if it wasn't for our general fear of our own mechs during the war, we could have won. Arla was a big part of that—the fear, that is."

Kora shrugged. "Maybe. I was just a kid then, I didn't have a real good view of what was going on."

Tremon had never checked Kora's age, and was

surprised to see that she was only twenty-five. She had the eyes of a hundred-year-old, though that was common amongst much of the younger generation who had grown up during the war.

"You from the Genevia System?" he asked.

"No," Kora shook her head. "From Gerra. Always thought about going back, but if what we hear from that captain on the *Slythe* is true, I should count my lucky stars that I didn't."

"Niets," Tremon muttered. "They claim to be a master race, but it's more like they ran a breeding program for assholes."

"Yeah, that's for sure. The PD in Jague isn't sure what to do now that we don't have the Niets barking orders. Taking a lot of headspace to make the adjustment."

"I can imagine. So, if Arla was a bigwig in a multi-system resistance, that means she's going to have a lot of loyalists—and we might have just pissed off the people who'd be our best allies."

"I'm going to try to suss that out," Kora said. "I've got a few contacts who might be able to put me in touch with the resistance members that brought her insystem."

"I'll get you in touch with Gary and Annie," Tremon added. "Annie has been working insystem for some time, she might have known some other operatives. Gary worked top-side security at the Refuge, so he had to have been privy to a lot of the comings and goings there. If there's a larger resistance network across the nearby stars, we're going to need to know who to work with when we show up to rescue them."

"How's that going?"

"Well, you'll be happy to know that Captain Travis is leading a seven-ship battlegroup to Gerra, and we're prepping fleets to jump to Burroughs, Oran, and Morres. Nothing huge, but hopefully enough to scare off the Niets before they make too big a mess."

"What about Genevia?" Kora asked. "I heard that we were worried the Niets would do a drive-by on the outer system if we depleted our forces here too much."

Tremon glanced at Kora, impressed that she seemed to know everything that was going on—or nearly everything.

"There's a surprise waiting for them if they try that, but Rika's ordered me to keep it hush-hush."

The detective laughed. "Well, far be it from me to run afoul of our new queen."

"You know she hates that, right?"

Kora snorted. " 'Queen' is a thousand times better than 'magnus'. She should be thanking us."

"I'll be sure to let her know that," Tremon replied, surprised at how certain he felt that Rika would survive whatever was going on around Babylon. "I've sent a message to Gary. He's here at the estate, if you want to meet him. Annie's on her way out to the heliopause jump gates, so might take a bit longer to hear back from her."

Kora nodded and turned to walk away. "Thanks for the intros. I'll get the intel we need, don't worry."

The chancellor snorted. "What's there to worry about?"

THE RIGHT CHOICE

STELLAR DATE: 06.03.8950 (Adjusted Years)
LOCATION: Corinth City, Chad
REGION: Burroughs System, Old Genevia, Nietzschean Empire

<*OK, so the garbage guy's next stop is two blocks from where the tow is going,*> Gero announced a few minutes later, breaking the silence that had stretched between Rajiz and Avi. <*I'm not sure if you can get over there in time.*>

<*Wait, what?*> Rajiz sat up straight, a scowl forming on his brow. <*Where's Betty?*>

<*Ummm…well, she **was** in position, but I haven't been able to raise her for the past five minutes.*>

<*Gero…*> the captain fumed. <*When were you planning on telling me this?*>

The engineer made a sound like he was sucking in a nervous breath. <*I was hoping never, thought maybe she was just taking a piss or something.*>

<*Leaving,*> Avi corrected. <*You leave piss, you don't take it.*>

<*Shut up, Avi,*> Rajiz and Gero said in unison.

<*Betty,*> Rajiz called out to the *ViperTalon*'s muscle. <*You need to get the case out of that truck. Gonna be mighty suspicious if Avi and I stroll on by.*>

There was no response, and the captain closed his eyes for a moment, begging the stars to give him patience.

<*Fine!*> he growled. <*You can paint your cabin any way you want.*>

<*Hot pink it is! And the crew passageway?*> Betty's meek tone stood in stark contrast to everything around them.

<*Don't push your luck. The Niets are gonna raze this planet, and you're gonna want a ride into the black before that happens.*>

<*Fiiiiiine. I'm in position, by the way. Just popped into a shop that sold these little dolls. They were super cute.*>

<*Please focus, Betty.*>

<*I'm built out of focus.*>

That was about the furthest thing from the truth, but Rajiz didn't push the issue. <*OK. We're pulling up to the garage now. I'll have to sign the groundcar over, and then we'll meet you at the rendezvous.*>

<*You got it, Boss. I see the stink truck coming. How did I get this part of the job anyway?*>

Avi snorted. <*Because the Niets would shoot you before letting you into their compound.*>

<*Oh, yeah, I guess there's that.*>

<*Focus,*> Rajiz said again, giving Avi a quelling look as the tower stopped and the pair got out. "Don't rile her up."

"I'd never do something like that."

"If by 'never', you're using an alternate definition that means always…."

Avi placed a hand over her chest. "You malign me, Captain,"

"Occupational hazard," Rajiz said absently as a mechanic came out of the shop and handed him a tablet.

The captain authed with it and passed a secure token indicating acknowledgment of transfer to the repair shop.

"Breaking groundcars is a hazard?" the mechanic asked with a quirked eyebrow.

"Could be," Rajiz gave a noncommittal shrug. "Depends on where they break."

The mechanic grunted in response and then waved to the tow driver to drop the groundcar next to two others.

The pair of thieves turned and walked down the street toward the rendezvous, keeping their movements casual as they passed by the few pedestrians in the commercial area that lay to the north of the spaceport.

"Oh, now that smells good," Avi said as they walked past a small coffee shop. "I haven't eaten all day."

"Whose fault is that?" Rajiz asked. "We're on a schedule here. No time for donuts."

Avi gave him a measuring look. "It's like I don't even know you! We have a seven-minute buffer, we can get donuts."

He switched to the Link. <*The buffer is for emergencies.*>

<*Which is what this is. A donut emergency.*>

<*I'll take a crème-filled one, if they have any,*> Gero chimed in.

<*And a strawberry-frosted for me,*> Betty added. <*No, make that six strawberry-frosted.*>

Rajiz groaned as Avi made a hard right and walked

into the donut shop.

<What did I say, Betty? You need to focus.>

<I'll focus better knowing there are donuts waiting for me. Besides, I already got the case.>

<You what? How?>

<Easy, I hopped onto the back of the truck as it drove by and grabbed it before the stinker even got to its next stop. By the way, Avi, next time try not to throw it next to…stars, I don't even know what that was. Do the Niets eat horses or something?>

<Shit, Betty,> Avi hissed. *<That was just commissary waste.>*

<Smelled like dead horse.>

<Say that again and you get zero donuts.>

<It was a field of roses.>

"I'll take two glazed," Rajiz said to Avi before responding to Betty. *<Great, just get your metal ass to the rendezvous already.>*

<Double-timing it. I'm highly motivated by food, you know.>

<Oh, I know.>

Five minutes later, the pair was approaching the rendezvous, a four-story automated carpark, with a bag of donuts and a tray of coffees. As annoyed as Rajiz was with Avi and her never-ending need for carbs and caffeine, he had to admit that the stop would allay any suspicion, should the Niets review surveillance when the theft was noticed—if it ever was.

As they approached the building, Avi glanced his

way. "Admit it, Captain, these are good donuts."

He looked down at the half-eaten glazed in his hand. "OK…yeah, they're not bad."

"Not bad? It's like heaven in a little circle."

Rajiz only laughed in response as he passed a command to the carpark to have their vehicle brought down to the ground level.

<Uh…Captain?>

Betty's tone carried a heavy dose of concern, and Rajiz tensed, his gaze sweeping across the intersection, noting two groundcars, one aircar, and four pedestrians all alone.

<What is it?>

<I'm being followed,> Betty replied. *<Not sure by who yet. A pair of people. Kinda small, but maybe dangerous.>*

<How far away are you?>

<A block, just turning the corner.>

The captain turned and saw Betty come into view, her large frame and loping stride giving her away—something that was unavoidable with her four legs.

Other ship captains regularly questioned his sanity for bringing a literal centaur on as crew. As often as not, he questioned his own sanity right along with them. But when push came to shove, no one kicked ass in a fight like Betty.

The horse part of her body was a combination of cybernetic and organic—mostly machine underneath and skin on top, though a second set of organs operated inside to keep blood clean and flowing through her hide.

From the waist up, she appeared to be a normal woman…if you didn't count the mane that grew down her back. She rarely wore clothing of any sort, though on Chad, modesty laws demanded that she cover her breasts, which she did with cups that magnetically attached to mount points on her chest.

If he were honest with himself, the fact that she was both majestic and beautiful fed into Rajiz's decision to hire her—even if it did cost a fortune to buy the specialized armor and EV gear she required.

A sling hung across her back, and he could see the case's profile inside as it bounced against her flank. The captain breathed a sigh of relief, knowing that if he could get it to the buyer, he'd be flush with food and fuel for the foreseeable future.

The roofless groundcar with a wide open bed in the back settled down next to Avi, and she got in the driver's seat.

"Slide over," he directed, and she shook her head.

"You shoot better than you drive, Captain."

He jumped into the back and then slid into the front passenger seat. "I don't know about that, but I sure shoot better than you do."

"Guns are under the seat." Avi activated manual driving mode and pulled out onto the street, driving at a leisurely pace toward Betty. <*Get ready to hop in.*>

<*I was born ready,*> Betty replied. <*But I'll stay on my hooves for a bit.*>

The centaur was twenty meters away from the car,

and as the vehicle approached, she reached into the pouch on her back and grabbed the case, casually tossing it into the back of the groundcar as it passed.

A second after it landed in the vehicle's bed, two large men rounded the corner.

"She needs to work on her definition of 'kinda small'," Avi muttered. "Their biceps are the size of my waist."

Rajiz shrugged. "When you're three meters tall, you tend to see things differently."

"I suppose," Avi muttered as she drove past the two men tailing Betty. "The real question is why I haven't mentally adjusted to how she describes people yet."

"Yeah, she's been crew for three years now. More than enough ti—"

One of the two thugs following Betty glanced at the back of the groundcar as they passed, and his eyes widened as he spotted the case.

"Hey!" he shouted. "Stop!"

"Your mom!" Avi yelled back and punched the accelerator.

" 'Your mom'?" Rajiz asked as he lifted his rifle, training it on the two men as the car sped away.

One of the thugs pulled a pistol from inside his jacket, and Rajiz fired a pulse blast, the concussive wave only causing the man to stagger slightly.

That's all the delay they needed.

A second later, a voice screamed "Yeeehaw!" and Betty smashed into the thug, a hind hoof flashing out and catching the other in the gut as she ran past.

"Suckers!" she added while galloping toward the groundcar.

One of the men was back on his feet in a second, but Betty pulled a pair of pistols from her pouch and opened fire on him, a focused pulse blast driving the thug to his knees.

Then the groundcar rounded the corner, and he lost sight of the thugs and Betty.

"Slow down." He waved a hand at Avi.

"She can run almost as fast as this thing's top speed," the first mate replied, maintaining her pace.

Sure enough, a second later, Betty rounded the corner, half twisted with both guns firing, a gleeful laugh filling the air.

"Oh hell yeah!"

"Just get in the car already," Rajiz said, but the centaur shook her head.

"No way!" She galloped closer and tossed her two pistols into the car's bed, and pulled a rifle from her pouch, opening fire on the corner just as the two men came around it.

The weapon spewed small pellets that dissolved in the air while flying toward their target, turning into viscous balls of liquid. They were non-lethal, but hit with enough force to leave serious welts.

One of the men went down, and the other ducked back around the corner.

"Shoot, I think I hit him in the eye," Betty said as she

drew even with the car.

"*Now* will you get in?" he demanded.

"Fiiiiiine." With surprising grace for someone her size, the centaur hopped into the back of the vehicle and crouched down as best she could.

"Why are they chasing you?" Avi asked as they turned onto another street, this one busier, allowing them to blend in with traffic.

"Other than the fact that we used their truck to mule something for us, or maybe it's that they probably didn't even know that and think we stole from them?" Betty asked.

<*Looks like those two were from the PLI gang,*> Gero chimed in. <*Not the same group as our truck driver friend works for, a bit higher up the chain.*>

<*Gonna give us trouble, you think?*> Rajiz asked.

<*So long as they don't ID us, we should be fine,*> Betty said.

<*They saw us,*> Avi muttered. <*They're gonna ID us.*>

<*As employees of Starlight Technical,*> Gero replied. <*Well, the captain and first mate. So far as I can tell, you might be the only centaur on Chad, Betty.*>

Rajiz shared a look with Avi, and she picked up the pace, moving onto an expressway that led to the spaceport's main entrance. For all the usefulness of having Betty on the crew, she was easy to ID and not at all hard to track back to the *ViperTalon.*

<*Good thing I used my kitty carrier to get off the ship,*> Betty said, referring to the crate she'd occupied, which

had been delivered to a warehouse near the rendezvous the day before.

<*Doesn't help us much now, though,*> Avi countered.

Rajiz considered the contingency plans he'd put together. One involved getting Betty to a waiting shipping container, another involved getting the whole team to shipping containers, and the third involved just driving right up to the ship and flying off.

Granted, that was the plan for when the people chasing them were not part of one of the most powerful crime rings on Chad.

"Just had to be the PLI," he muttered.

"Should have gone with my seduction plan," Avi said. "It's not failed us yet."

"Maybe I should have," the captain said, glancing back at the case that sat next to Betty. "Live and learn."

The first mate banked onto an off-ramp and then took the first exit on the next road, skirting the passenger terminals, and angling toward the long rows of commercial cradles.

The rows of ships went on for three kilometers, and the group was halfway to theirs when a message hit Rajiz's Link. He didn't recognize the person reaching out, and considered ignoring it, but the message was tagged urgent by the spaceport's routing system, so he grudgingly accepted.

<*Rajiz, captain of the* ViperTalon. *What can I do for you?*>

<*I know who you are,*> the voice said.

The message came with no ident, not even a pseudonym accompanying it. A knot began to form in the captain's stomach.

<*I suppose that makes one of us,*> he said.

<*Who I am is not important. The fact that I represent the PLI is.*>

"Fuck," he muttered.

"What is it?" Avi asked.

"PLI connected the dots. Probably going to have to pay them off."

"With what?" she gave him a worried glance.

"I'll think of something." He drew in a steadying breath and released it slowly before replying. <*Look, we didn't take anything of yours, we just used the truck to mule something out for us.*>

<*That's not really giving me the warm fuzzies,*> the voice on the other end of the Link said. <*I think you owe us a transportation fee, as well as compensation for the pain and suffering you caused our people.*>

Rajiz resisted letting out a long groan. <*Maybe you need to hire better people.*>

<*I'll admit, I'm not happy with their performance. How's about I let you keep whatever you lifted from the Niets, and you strongly encourage your horse lady to sign on with the PLI?*>

<*Convincing her to stay on Chad is going to be a hard sell. Do you have any off-world locations she could go to?*>

Rajiz's sarcastic tone seemed to catch the gangster by surprise.

<Sorry…what?>

<You need to tell your truck driver to pay more attention. The Niets are preparing to leave Chad.>

<All the more reason to stay. Opportunity is gonna abound.>

<They were readying a wing of Razers.>

The words crossed the Link, and a leaden silence followed.

<Shit,> the voice muttered. *<That's sooner than we expected.>*

<You ***expected*** *this?>*

<OK, buddy, here's how it's going to go. You work for us now. A rep will be by your ship in half an hour to talk to you about your first job.>

Rajiz couldn't help but laugh, both aloud and over the Link. *<We'll be gone by then.>*

<No you won't. Port's grounded you. Check your status.>

<Aww shit,> the *Talon*'s captain muttered. *<You've got more pull here than I thought.>*

<Yeah, so don't try anything, or your ship is going to be on the receiving end of a permanent solution.>

<You need to work on your recruitment pitch.>

The connection dropped, and Rajiz slumped in his seat.

"That bad?" Avi asked.

"That bad." He nodded. "Our new employers are going to send someone to meet with us in a bit."

"Our what?" Betty's head was suddenly in the front row. "What just happened?"

"The PLI has…hired us," Rajiz replied. "Don't worry. They clearly want our ship for something, so we just have to smile and nod, and then get the hell out of Burroughs as soon as we can."

Avi snorted. "Run away. I like it, that's more our style."

"It's not—" Rajiz began to protest, but both Avi and Betty fixed him with cold stares. "OK…maybe it is, but it keeps us alive."

"Hey, not complaining," Avi said. "I like being alive. Just calling a spade a spade."

SCOURING

STELLAR DATE: 06.03.8950 (Adjusted Years)
LOCATION: GMS *Pinnacle,* Babylon
REGION: Genevia System, New Genevian Alliance

"We keep searching till we're certain," Rika ordered. "I'm not going to be the one that loses a stasis shield system and screws the war for the Alliance."

"Stars, Rika, the *Lance*'s generators are probably on their way to Babylon's core by now," Heather muttered. "Along with the rest of my girl."

Rika gave the captain a sympathetic look. The *Lance* had been her flagship for nearly two years, a symbol of Marauder strength to see Genevians flying a new—and rather powerful—Nietzschean warship, snatched away from the enemy in the Hercules System.

"I feel it too," the magnus said. "She was home. The best home we've ever had."

<*It was comfy,*> Niki chimed in, laughing softly.

"What do you mean by that?" Rika asked.

<*No idea, just thought I'd add something.*>

Rika groaned and glanced at Heather, whose eyes were misty.

"I never thought I'd captain a ship like that." The other woman's voice was barely audible. "Being a mech…it…well, you know."

"And now look at you." Rika placed a hand on her

friend's shoulder. "You went from a top-of-the line Nietzschean dreadnought to now captaining their most powerful superweapon-ship."

"Bigger isn't always better. This thing handles like a garbage scow, which makes sense since we're lugging a black hole around."

Rika snorted. "The *Lance* wasn't a ballerina, either, you know."

"Not even a day gone, and you're besmirching my precious *Fury Lance*!" Heather exclaimed in mock anger—at least, Rika thought the statement was meant to be humorous.

"I'll never besmirch the *Lance.* Trust me. I'm mourning both it, and all the gear we left behind."

"The ISF is going to be pissed. They just got us that QuanComm blade. We're cut off again."

A sigh slipped past Rika's lips. "Story of my life. At least Tangel is OK. I didn't get all the details from Carson before he had to leave, but he said she's alive, and that her internal QC was taken out by something or another that he didn't fully understand himself."

"Well, OK, so long as New Canaan isn't destroyed," Heather said. "Who would attack the ISF's home system? I heard that their government had re-authorized the use of picobombs."

<*Took them long enough,*> Niki said.

"I hope we find out soon," Rika replied. "Having Carson's fleet back will solve about a thousand different problems."

"You know we can't count on that happening," Heather replied. "We have to assume the worst."

Rika shook her head, brow lowered. "No, that's not how I operate. I'll *prepare* for the worst, but I'm going to believe in the best until I see otherwise."

"Ma'am," Chief Ona looked up from her console. "I think we have it! There's a section of the *Lance* in orbit a hundred klicks below us. If the decks within aren't mashed up, it'll have one of the stasis generators inside."

"Good work, Chief," Heather said. "Coordinate with Bondo, and get drones down there to see if we can pull it out."

Rika smiled at the captain. "See? One down, two to go. We'll get them installed in the *Pinnacle*, and be on our way."

"About that..." Heather said. "How do you feel about renaming this ship? '*Pinnacle*' is so...pretentious."

"And '*Fury Lance*' wasn't? Niets are always a bit snooty with their ship names."

"Again with besmirching my precious *Lance*. We kept the name because it was badass."

"And we were kinda busy," Rika added. "Fighting off a bajillion Niets around Pyra, if I recall."

Heather nodded. "Sure, yeah. So, since there aren't bajillion Niets to fight off right now, what do you think of naming this ship the... *Death Spear*?"

"Stars, Heather, no. That's a terrible name."

"*Starkiller*?"

"Nuh uh."

"Perilous Strike?"

"Not terrible, but still no."

A grin formed on Heather's lips and she thrust a finger in the air. *"The Even More Furious Lance!"*

<*Stars! So much bad,*> Niki groaned.

"Lance of the Marauders?"

"Hmmmm." Rika tapped her chin. "That's got some promise. What about the *Marauders' Lance*?"

A grin split Heather's lips. "I knew you'd come around."

"You gave me those shitty options at first so we could land here, didn't you?" Rika asked.

"Again with the besmirching!" Heather proclaimed.

"You need a new word."

NEW EMPLOYER

STELLAR DATE: 06.03.8950 (Adjusted Years)
LOCATION: Corinth City Spaceport, Chad
REGION: Burroughs System, Old Genevia, Nietzschean Empire

The groundcar was stowed in the aft hold, and the crew had taken up positions in the corridor that ran along the starboard side of the ship, one deck above the keel.

Rajiz stood at the mid-ship starboard airlock, where a long ramp curved to the walkway below. A walkway being traversed by two hulking thugs and a slender woman.

<*They the same meatheads I took down?*> Betty asked. <*I can't really tell. All you bipeds look the same to me.*>

<*Funny,*> Avi snorted. <*And no, they look like new meatheads.*>

<*People like this usually have an unlimited supply of generic thugs,*> Gero commented. <*Ever notice that?*>

<*Yeah, so expect there to be a lot more than just these two out there,*> the captain replied. <*Now shut it. I need to concentrate.*>

<*On the woman?*> Betty sent a smirk over the shipnet. <*She sure is purty.*>

<*Quiet.*>

The woman certainly was attractive, but she wasn't Rajiz's type, so resisting her charms—should she choose to use them—wouldn't be problematic.

He folded his arms behind his back and waited for the PLI's envoy to climb the ramp. The woman's eyes met his when she was halfway up, and her unblinking gaze never wavered from that point on. When she finally stopped a meter before him, a mirthless smile formed on her lips.

"Captain Rajiz. Welcome to the PLI."

"Let's not be hasty," he replied, extending a hand, which she clasped and gave a single shake before releasing. "I don't even know your name. I like to have one of those before doing business with someone."

"Rachella," she replied. "I represent the PLI's acquisitions arm. We're always looking to bring new crews onboard, expand our reach, you know…fun stuff."

"The only fun stuff I'm interested in is getting out of here before the Niets flatten the place."

"May I come in?" Rachella asked. "I really don't fancy having this chat out in the open. If the Niets find out that we know about their plans, they'll up the timetable, and that's not good for either of us."

Rajiz shrugged. He suspected she was right, and gestured for her to enter the ship. "Just you, though. Your meat boys can stay out here."

"Meat boys?" one of them protested.

"Easy, Jim," Rachella said gently. "He's not going to do anything stupid. Not if he wants this ship to ever lift off again."

"Yeah, Jim," Rajiz said. "I'm not stupid."

"Then why'd you call us meat boys? That's pretty stupid."

"Don't make me send Betty out to trample you." The captain grinned, then followed Rachella as she walked through the airlock and onto the ship, turning toward the bow and continuing down the passage a dozen meters.

Her false smile disappeared, and she fixed Rajiz with a serious look. "It's clear that you're just passing by, looking to make a buck, but let me explain something about Chad. The PLI runs it, not the Niets. We've got things going pretty good here, and we want to keep it that way."

"Good luck," Rajiz replied. "I fought in the war. Niets didn't pull out often, but when they did, they didn't do it nicely. Sore losers."

Rachella's gaze grew distant. "Yeah, that's one word for it."

"So let me see if I can skip a few steps. You're a front organization for a resistance, and since there's no real way to resist the Niets when they can just roll up on Chad and nuke it to shit, you've worked out a bit of an arrangement to keep things copacetic." Rachella's lips had drawn into a thin line as Rajiz spoke, and he couldn't help but smirk. "How am I doing?"

"Close enough," she replied, feigning indifference.

"But really, unless you've got your own fleet tucked away somewhere, what are you going to do? Time to cut your losses and get out."

"That's just the thing," the PLI woman said. "If the Niets wanted to wipe us out, they'd just nuke us, or roast the planet with their engines. But you said they're prepping Razers, which means they want to make things messy, but not totally wipe us out."

"Shit," Rajiz muttered, thinking of the news coming out of Genevia. "They want to make us into a problem."

"Yeah, for Rika and the Marauders."

"Those the mercs who took Genevia? Is it true they killed the emperor?"

"Seems like it," Rachella nodded. "Colonel Rika and her fleet have been slicing through Genevia for months now. Their last stop was in Iberia, and no one expected them to show up in Genevia right afterward—least of all the Niets, it seems."

For the first time, the woman gave a genuine laugh, and Rajiz wondered if she and the PLI really were true believers in freedom, not just opportunists.

"OK," he shrugged. "So some mercs took Genevia—and a few other systems. Just a few hundred to go then, eh? They're a long way from actually defeating the Niets."

"Those mercs are backed by some powerful allies," Rachella said. "Just one Marauder ship is a match for dozens of Nietzschean cruisers."

Rajiz suddenly realized where she was going. "You want the *ViperTalon* to go to Genevia and get these mercs to come help Chad."

"I knew you were smarter than you looked,"

Rachella's lips formed a less-than-pleasant smile.

"Yeah, well, you're not. We're deep in Burroughs' gravity well. Even if we burn haaaard, we're looking at four days to get to a jump point, and the Niets haven't interdicted jumps to Genevia yet, but I bet they will soon, and they'll sure be curious about a ship boosting like mad to get there."

"Yes, well—" Rachella began, but Rajiz cut her off.

"And then it'll take the mercs four or five days to get to a jump point for Chad—that's *if* they decide to come help—and then another three or four to get insystem here. Let's say they've got some serious burners on their ships. You're looking at twelve days best-case, probably closer to fifteen. Face it, PLI woman, you're screwed."

"Stars, man. Will you let me get a word in edgewise?"

<*Oh…you made her mad!*> Avi chuckled in Rajiz's mind.

<*What did I tell you about interrupting?*>

<*Just let me know when I can shoot her.*>

Rajiz ignored his first mate, and nodded for Rachella to say her piece.

"Yes, I get that time is short, which is why we need to get you on the move. There's a shortcut to jump outsystem from here, only three AU away. It's only open for another two days, then it's obstructed by dark matter for a month. It'll take you four days to get to Genevia, and then one day for them to get back here."

"Seriously?" Rajiz asked. "One day? What sort of FTL do they have?"

"Some gate system," the woman replied with a shrug. "The Niets have them too…or one of their allies does. It's hard to be sure. Either way, there are a whole whack of these ring things in Genevia, most of them in the outer system, but a few around Belgium."

"Did the mercs bring them?"

"No, our intel on the rings is from before the Marauders showed up."

"OK, so let's say I do this little courier run for you." Rajiz leant against the bulkhead. "What's to stop me from just buggering off and leaving you in the lurch?"

"Well, for starters, I'm coming with you."

<Figures,> Gero commented. *<Just when I get my favorite beer in the larder, we have guests.>*

"And," Rachella continued, "my 'meat boys' are coming as well."

"Yeah, that's a big no," Rajiz shook his head. "I don't need them drinking all our beer. Besides, they're not going to be able to do much to help you out, anyway."

<Thank you, Captain,> the engineer replied. *<I always knew your heart was in the right place.>*

"Really?" Rachella cocked an eyebrow. "Jim and Jerry are combat vets. Don't underestimate them."

"And don't underestimate a fully armored centaur barreling through the corridors," Rajiz countered. "Trust me. We've been boarded before. It didn't go well for the other side."

"Colonel Rajiz of the Genevian Armed Forces, I thought you had more honor than that."

Rajiz drew himself up straight, his dark eyes boring into Rachella's green ones. "Don't you call me that. Don't you ever say those words again. You do, and I'll kill you where you stand, meat boys or no meat boys."

A deafening silence followed as the pair stared at one another for over a minute. Finally, Rachella broke eye contact and took a step back.

"Fine. We'll do this a different way. From what I hear, you owe Kershaw in the Morres System a nice sum of credit. You do this, and we'll square it away for you."

"And what if the Niets burn Chad to a cinder before we get back?"

"We have off-world funds," she explained. "So long as they don't trash the whole system, we'll be able to make good on our promise."

"And no meat boys?"

"Nice try. Jim and Jerry are non-negotiable. Besides, I thought you put your faith in Betty and her armor."

Rajiz set his jaw, and glowered at Rachella, wishing he'd gone with Avi's seduction plan at the Nietzschean compound.

"Fine. Show me the charts with this dark layer shortcut."

A MEET AND A MISSION

STELLAR DATE: 06.03.8950 (Adjusted Years)
LOCATION: Mount Genevia, Belgium
REGION: Genevia System, New Genevian Alliance

"Well, Gary, what do you think?" Kora asked as the man's lips twisted in indecision. "We need to find who brought Arla to Belgium, and then find out if they were just a ride, or if the resistance in the surrounding systems is gonna resist Rika as much as the Niets."

"Yeah," the lieutenant nodded. "I get that, I really do, but this feels like rolling on people who have had my back for years."

"Sure," Kora nodded, "I can see how you'd feel that way. But let's be straight, here. I've only known of Rika for a couple of weeks, and it's clear as day to me that she's Genevia's future. Do you feel any differently?"

"No," Gary shook his head. "I agree with you in every way, that's why I sided with Rika against Oda back at the Refuge. Trust me, I'm not going to go against her now. But walking away from the Refuge, and pointing the finger at rebels isn't the same thing."

Kora rose from the chair she'd been sitting in and walked across the small meeting room in what was becoming known as the Royal Palace. She stood at the window for a moment, looking down at the forested slopes of Mount Genevia, before turning back to face

Gary, who had remained seated.

"And what of the mechs?" she asked. "Arla facilitated the use of the KK100. Not only that, but the Niets had one on the *Pinnacle*, too. Either she was working with the Nietzscheans, or she's complicit in some other way. Regardless, I need to get to the bottom of it all."

"You?" Gary cocked an eyebrow. "Why you?"

"Tremon gave me the task," Kora shrugged. "But even if he didn't, I'd be all over this. I'm not just going to sit back and let infighting tear down what the Marauders have done here. We have a chance at a real Genevia again. A strong nation, a united people."

"I'm with you." Gary nodded. "I really am, it's just…."

"It's just what?" she asked.

"Just going to make for a bit of self-loathing is all."

Kora pursed her lips, knowing all too well what the man meant. "If it makes you feel any better, I've had my fair share of that. I've been a cop here for years, just made it to detective a few months ago. This job…it's supposed to be to help people, but that wasn't so easy under the Niets. I did my best, but sometimes I had to make hard choices, weigh two evils."

"Yeah." Gary nodded. "That's what this feels like. Either way, I think I know where to start."

"Oh?" Kora asked, an encouraging smile settling on her lips. "Where to?"

Gary's gaze darted to the ceiling. "We need to get to Capeton Command. Annie introduced me to a guy there,

I think he'll know where to start digging."

"Can we just hit him up over the Link?" Kora asked.

"No." Gary shook his head. "He's not going to give us what we want without a bit of squeezing."

The detective laughed. "Luckily, I have a lot of on-the-job training when it comes to that."

"Stars…just don't make me regret this too much."

Kora patted Gary on the shoulder. "Don't worry, I'll keep your delicate feelings firmly in mind."

TALONFLIGHT

STELLAR DATE: 06.03.8950 (Adjusted Years)
LOCATION: *ViperTalon*, near Chad
REGION: Burroughs System, Old Genevia, Nietzschean Empire

Rajiz shifted in his captain's chair, eyeing Rachella, the unwelcome guest on his bridge. The rail-thin woman sat at the auxiliary console to Avi's left, doing her best to annoy the hell out of him.

Granted, the PLI babysitter wasn't actually doing anything specific, but the way she sat with her shoulders back and her straight, blonde hair falling down over the back of the seat seemed like a calculated measure designed just to piss him off.

Stars, man, relax!

"We've got clearance to transition out of orbit on our assigned vector," Avi said, throwing a worried glance in Rajiz's direction. "We'll be able to burn on it for two hours, but then we're going to have to break off to make for our secret jump point."

"How secret is it, anyway?" the captain asked Rachella. "I mean, if you use it enough to map it, the Niets must have spotted ships dropping out there."

"We're real careful," she replied with a noncommittal shrug. "Plus, we make sure all the right people are paid off. Trust me, it's far from common knowledge."

"So when we veer off, the Niets are gonna do what?"

Avi asked.

Rachella sighed. "You're the savvy pirate ship, what would you use as your excuse for changing course?"

Rajiz had already been considering several options, and pointed at one of the two ice giants in the outer system. "We'll redeclare our vector to use Jujell as slingshot mass for fuel savings. They have a vector past the planet set up for that."

"A bit off from where we'll really be vectoring," Avi replied. "But I imagine they'll buy it. No one in this system really cares much if you burn straight or not."

"Works for me," Rachella said with a shrug. "Your *Talon* can outrun whatever they toss at us anyway, right?"

Rajiz had already reviewed the Nietzschean patrol craft in their general vicinity, and nodded. "Unless they send a relativistic missile our way, we're fine. And no way I can see them wasting something that expensive on us."

"So long as they don't know who you really are," Rachella said with a laugh. "I bet the Niets would love to stop you from robbing them in every system you go to."

"I have no idea what you're talking about," he replied.

The bridge fell silent once more, and Rajiz decided to kill time by reviewing all of the ships' systems. Something in his gut told him that they were going on more than just a milk run.

He hadn't asked Rachella why the PLI had decided to

use a new and unknown person for such an important mission—mostly because he didn't want a bullshit answer—but there had to be a reason. It was likely to do with not connecting their surreptitious exit with any known PLI craft, or maybe it was that the gangsters weren't as big a going concern as they liked to pretend, and they had no ships of their own.

Either way, he felt half good for doing the right thing in helping his fellow Genevians against the Niets, and half like an idiot for getting mixed up with a local rebel group…again.

Not going to be like last time, he thought. *We get to Genevia, Rachella delivers her message, and the mercenaries use their fancy jump gates to get back to Burroughs.*

Of course, he knew it wasn't that simple. He still had to turn around and go back as well, to get his payment.

Unless I just forgo that and drop Rachella and her meat boys on whatever station is nearby.

The situation made Rajiz want to scream.

He'd long since given up caring about his former nation of Genevia. They'd lost, and their systems now belonged to Nietzschea. For a time, he'd fought against the occupiers, but all that ended up doing was getting good people killed.

After a few years of struggle, he'd come to realize that the war had already taken too many lives. Resisting just made the Niets grind their oppressor's boot into the remaining Genevians even harder.

Best to just get on with life.

A wave of guilt washed over Rajiz as he considered that while he'd given in and gone along with the flow, others had continued to fight back—and rather successfully, if the PLI and reports out of the Genevia System were to be believed.

He'd always told himself that his raids on Nietzschean facilities were his way of striking back—a way that put few others at risk, and kept his ship in fuel and food.

But the feeling that he'd dropped out of the rebellion too soon had been nagging at him ever since he'd heard the first rumors that some sort of mercenary force had attacked Genevia. Another part of him knew what that really meant, what was really going to happen now.

The war was back on, and the people caught in the crossfire were going to be those least able to defend themselves.

The razing of Chad would be just the beginning. If the Niets were actually retreating, they would shred the Genevian systems on their way out. There would barely be enough to rebuild with.

Stars…didn't you used to be an optimist?

He reminded himself that his initial plan had been to review ships systems, with the goal of keeping his mind from wandering through such unpleasant topics. He returned to that, checking over the *ViperTalon*'s shields, main weapons—a set of ten-centimeter beams aft, and fifteens up front—and the smaller kinetic and point defense systems.

Everything checked out, and he switched to reviewing the engine profile, monitoring its burn and efficiency numbers. Gero would have alerted him to any issues with the drive system, but Rajiz knew that a good captain had an eye on everything, anticipating any issues their crew might raise.

The fusion burners were running clean, happily sipping on their optimal mix of deuterium and tritium. A small store of antimatter waited in the annihilation chamber, should they decide to activate the antimatter-pion drive.

Rachella had already expressed a strong desire for them to do so, but Rajiz had explained that no one burned AP on ships like the *ViperTalon* unless they were up to no good, or moving something very expensive—which was usually the same thing. Spewing gamma wash behind the freighter would just make the Niets pay a lot more attention to a single ship amongst hundreds of thousands of others.

His review brought up a few systems that needed repairs, a scan array that was running on a secondary antenna, the port-side airlock that would jam if they used it in atmo, and three rather unsightly gashes in the forward ablative plating from encounters with people who didn't feel the same way Rajiz did about their property.

The usual.

Regardless of whether or not some mercs were running around liberating systems, Kershaw would still be king of the heap in Morres, and Rajiz looked forward to paying him off. Then he could finally fix those annoying issues on the *Talon* and get his girl in tip-top condition.

Maybe he could finally find courier commissions that would get him out of Old Genevia, and he could leave this mess behind. Find greener pastures in Septhia, or perhaps even the ASN Coalition.

"I'm going for a walk," he said, rising from his chair. "Let me know when you're going to alter course."

"You got it, Boss." Avi nodded without turning, and Rachella didn't even give that much of an acknowledgment.

A tour of the ship—which took him past the galley were Betty had challenged Jim and Jerry to a drinking contest, and then past the engineering bay where Gero floated immersed in a VR field, his arms flapping awkwardly—did little to quell Rajiz's angst, and before long, he found himself back on the bridge shortly after Avi had brought the ship onto their outsystem vector.

"I did what I could, you know," he said to Rachella, walking around her console to stand before the woman. "I fought. I fought for ten years in the war, and four afterward. I lost—" his voice cut out.

"Everyone," Rachella said quietly. "I know…I did too. Stars, everyone lost pretty much everyone. We're all still putting it together again after that shitshow of a war."

"Fuuuuck." Rajiz leant back against the bulkhead.

"You got new people, Boss," Avi said. "We all lost,

too. You know that. Now we have a new family."

"I know," he replied, drawing in a slow breath. "Still miss the old one—though it hurts less, having you dorks around."

"Wow, can you feel the—shit, now what?"

Rajiz folded his arms across his chest, fingers drumming on a forearm as he waited for Avi to elaborate.

"Niets changed their minds," she said after a minute. "They're denying our slingshot passage around Jujell and are ordering us back onto our prior vector."

Rachella's eyebrows lifted as she regarded him, but the PLI woman didn't speak, only watched intently as he pushed himself away from the bulkhead and ran a hand through his hair.

"Send them an acknowledgment, Avi. Tell them we're plotting a burn to get us on the other vector without pissing away a ton of fuel."

"Will do. I assume we're just buying time?"

"Yeah, as much as we can before they send someone after us."

"Do you think they will?" Rachella asked.

Rajiz brought up a holodisplay showing one AU of space around the *ViperTalon.* Chad and its smattering of space stations were near the bottom of the holo, and a few dozen freighters were dotted throughout the area. Other than a few cruisers in low orbit around Chad, the only other Nietzschean ships in the area were a pair of small patrol boats, both roughly the same size as the

Talon, though more heavily armed.

One was seven light minutes away, but the other's patrol route had brought it much closer than expected, only three light minutes distant. They were Kalier Class ships, which theoretically could catch up to the *Talon,* but only if they burned antimatter to do it.

"You look worried," Rachella said. "I thought that none of the Niet ships could catch the *ViperTalon*."

"That's not exactly what I said. I didn't think they'd be in range to do it." He pointed at the closer of the two patrol craft. "That one could, if they really pour it on. Normally I'd wager against them bothering, they'd just have a ship in the outer system intercept us, but with the attack on Genevia, they might be feeling twitchy."

"Great," Avi muttered. "Twitchy Niets, my favorite."

Rajiz flagged the jump point on the holo. "We just have to make it here. That's twenty-eight light minutes as the photon flies." He glanced at Avi. "The second that Nietzschean jalopy shifts vector toward us, you spin out the AP drive and go max burn. I don't care how suspicious it's gonna look, I don't want them getting close."

"So, depending on if and when they do that, we're about eleven hours to jump," Rachella said.

" 'Bout that." Rajiz nodded. "Time for the best part of spaceflight. Waiting."

* * * * *

"T-minus fifteen!" Avi called out. "Those bastards are

closing, though."

<*Gero!*> Rajiz called down to engineering. <*Get that spare antimatter you keep tucked away and load it up. We need another burn from the AP drive!*>

<*Spare what, Boss? I—*>

<*If you give me any shit, I'm going to dump* ***you*** *in the reactor. Load it up!*>

There was a momentary pause, then the engineer responded. <*Right, on it.*>

"Wow, those Niets are getting really mad." Rachella was monitoring comms while Avi focused on jinking the ship to avoid incoming beamfire. "I bet there's foam and spittle flying everywhere."

"Niets tend to be more calm and cocksure, in my experience," Rajiz responded absently, keeping his focus on the jump point. "You're sure this route is good?"

"I'm on the ship, aren't I?" Rachella asked. "If I wasn't sure, I wouldn't be here, praying that we make it there before that ship back there carves a hole in our engines."

"They're good," Avi said. "I'll give them that. It's like they have our patterns."

"Just keep changing it up." Rajiz gave her an encouraging smile. "You're doing great."

"I'm not doing great," Avi muttered. "They've tagged our port engine cowling twice. One more, and they'll burn through and hit the bell."

"I've got a weird reading." Rachella highlighted a burst of static that was growing in intensity on a high band. "It's like another ship is out there. Niets don't have stealthed ships in Burroughs, though....do they?" She turned in her seat to look at Rajiz, and he pursed his lips.

"No. No they don't. That's an RM."

"Faaaaaawwwk!" Avi moaned. "We're still ten minutes from the point."

"The minute that missile is one light second out, you jink onto our final vector and dump to the dark layer," Rajiz ordered his first mate.

"What?! We'll still be at least three light seconds from dumping!"

Rajiz nodded. "Sure, but they always have some wiggle room on jump points."

"Yeah, sure, wiggle room on *official* ones. These shady-ass smuggler markers aren't on the official charts for a reason—no one wants to meet the long night in the DL!"

Rachella gestured to the marker showing the estimated position of the relativistic missile. "Yeah, well, we can either be sure about dying from that thing, or take a chance on the DL."

"Or we stop and surrender," Rajiz muttered, catching dark looks from the two women. "What? I had to say it."

"You know that at this point, the Niets will probably just let the RM do its job no matter what," Avi said.

"No," Rachella shook her head. "If they're willing to spend one of those on us, they'll want intel if we surrender. So...chalk that up as the worst possible outcome."

The ship lurched as she spoke, and Rajiz felt himself pressed back into his seat for a moment as the a-grav systems compensated for increased thrust.

<*OK, Boss, you owe me. That was my private stash.*>

<*You don't have a private stash, Gero,*> the captain replied. <*You siphoned off a bit of my official stash.*>

<*How is it a stash if it's official?*>

Rajiz groaned. <*Shut up, Gero. Just keep it humming, we're almost there.*>

"I wonder if anyone's ever made an RM that works in the dark layer," Rachella mused. "That would be really useful at times like this."

"Core, woman!" Avi grunted. "Don't say things like that. Going to give me waking nightmares or something."

"Too hard to control the entry vector," Rajiz said calmly. "It would overshoot its target, and then take forever to slow down with a-grav…as much as that works in the DL."

"Yeah," Avi sounded like she was grasping for serenity. "They'll probably bring it back around for recovery, if they don't get to…."

"Blow us to bits?" Rachella asked.

"Fuck!" Avi swore. "Seriously, woman, do you want me to have a panic attack and crash the ship?"

"Crash it into what?" Rachella gestured at the holo. "Other than the Niets and their missile, there's nothing out here."

Avi shot the PLI woman a dark look. "I'll find

something."

"We're picking up speed," Rajiz turned the conversation to a new topic. "Looks like we'll reach the point in seven minutes now."

"Yeah, well, I think they figured out our intended vector," Rachella said. "Look at the RM's jink pattern. It's stabilized, like they're focusing in."

Rajiz looked at the missile's most recent jinks and saw that, while it appeared to be matching the ship's vector, it was doing so from within a narrow cone, one that was centered on the jump point.

"Think they know about it?" he asked. "Or did we give it away?"

"We've never vectored in alignment with the marker," Avi said. "I'm not stupid."

"Yeah," Rachella agreed. "But you almost drew a circle around it with your jinking. They've got a good NSAI in that missile to pick up on it."

"Faaaaawk," Avi moaned again. "I did do that, shit. I practically drew a bullseye around the jump point."

The RM was tailing the *ViperTalon* by only three light seconds, and the ship was still several more from transition.

"Stay a quarter-degree off target," he said. "No more jinking. Then, when it gets to the one-second threshold, get on vector and dump."

"What about the patrol boat?" Avi asked.

"We pulled ahead with the AP burn. Their beams are only gonna tickle at this distance. Keep us spinning a touch, but nothing more."

Avi nodded and brought the ship onto a vector that was very nearly aligned with the jump point.

A tense minute passed on the bridge, all eyes on the scan data that gave the RM's position. It was as though the weapon was clawing its way through space, hungry and ready to devour its prey.

"You know," Rajiz said as the missile closed to within one-and-a-half light seconds. "This is not the first time this has happened to me, and it still sucks. I—"

An EM flare lit up on scan, and the *Talon*'s aft shields weakened, hammered by radiation from the explosion.

"They blew it so far away," Rachella muttered. "Why—"

"Avi! Get on course, dump now!"

"Aye!" the first mate called out, while Rachella turned and frowned at Rajiz.

"Why? They blew their load."

"The patrol boat," he stabbed a finger toward the craft. "Our shields are weak, it can punch through."

His words were emphasized by the deck bucking beneath their feet as the ship lurched, slewing to the side.

Then scan went dark.

SALVAGE

STELLAR DATE: 06.04.8950 (Adjusted Years)
LOCATION: GMS *Pinnacle,* Babylon
REGION: Genevia System, New Genevian Alliance

<*Second one is secure,*> Bondo called up. <*Gonna take us a bit to get it mounted in place, though.*>

<*I've analyzed the feeds from nearby stations,*> Piper chimed in. <*I can say with near-absolute certainty that the third stasis field generator is lost.*>

Rika considered the news, chewing on her lip as she watched Chief Ona and Heather coordinate with a salvage team from Hanging Gardens Station.

<*I suppose that's the best we can hope for, then. Getting two intact is more than I'd dreamt.*>

<*Not enough to make a full bubble around a ship this size, though,*> Bondo said. <*We're going to have to be careful.*>

Piper made a *hmmming* sound for a few seconds. <*I'm not entirely certain about that.*>

<*Oh? You think you've figured out ISF stasis tech?*> Bondo's tone contained a mixture of doubt and surprise.

<*I may have offered some pointers,*> Niki said in a smug voice. <*Honestly, I think it's kinda simple.*>

Bondo coughed. <*Negating the casimir effect at picoscale is simple?*>

<*Well, once you know it* ***can*** *be done, then you can start to dig a bit deeper into the how. The waveform the ISF system*

creates—along with its power requirements—rule out some theories and support others.>

<*Speaking of power options,*> Rika said. <*What about the CriEns? Have any been salvageable?*>

<*I have six that look decent,*> the chief engineer said. <*I'm going to have to do a full diagnostic and then test them on a static load and make sure they behave. Luckily, Orion gave the Niets zero point energy tech to power this behemoth.*>

<*Speaking of which…*> Worry had filtered into Niki's voice. <*I don't think this ship can successfully manage a dark layer transition. Not the way the graviton emitters are set up.*>

Rika ran a hand through her hair, jaw set, as she paced across the *Marauders' Lance*'s bridge. <*That's pretty freakin' annoying. How did the Niets expect to fly this thing around?*>

<*I think they planned to only use gates. Or maybe they were still working out how to jump a ship this big. Everyone thought six klicks was the limit until the* Intrepid *jumped out at Bollam's World, but now they know that's not true.*>

<*Funny that Orion never told them how,*> Piper said. <*I bet they know how to take larger ships through the DL.*>

Bondo snorted. <*I bet they were trying to keep a lid on the Niets. Garza controlled the jump gates here, and if the Niets couldn't take DMG ships into the dark layer, then they were dependent on Orion to move their fleets.*>

Rika had to admit that it sounded like something Garza would do. She'd only interacted with him briefly, but the man was a grade-A asshole, even if he was just a cloned asshole.

<*Good thing we had Carson's engineers on hand,*> Bondo added. <*Now we have twenty-three gates of our own, and mirrors on half our ships. The Marauders' teeth just got a bit sharper.*>

The conversation shifted to the timeline for the final collection of salvage—the oversight of which Rika planned to turn over to the pair of destroyers that would arrive in a few hours. She needed to get back to Belgium and organize the fleets that would head to Burroughs, Oran, and Morres.

Plus, she had to rescue Tremon from the snares of office. Though he was probably more capable than she at the civilian aspects of leadership, she knew that he didn't *want* to have the responsibility, and foisting it on him levied a feeling of guilt on her already-burdened conscience.

<*He doesn't mind as much as he puts on,*> Niki commented.

<*You're not supposed to do that.*>

<*I'm tired of pretending I can't read your mind. It's exhausting.*>

Rika let out a nervous laugh, earning her a look from Heather that she waved off. <*We've reached that stage, have we?*>

<*Yeah, though I have no idea if we're going to merge or not. Tanis and Angela had help from Bob and Earnest…plus the third quantum brain they constructed in their head. We don't have that, but our interconnectivity is creating…something.*>

The statement caused a nervous flutter in Rika's

stomach. <*Something? Like what?*>

<*I don't really know…I think it's transdimensional.*>

<*Great, just what I need right now, worry about ascending while we're trying to put Genevia back together.*>

<*Well, just don't get stuck in dire straits like Tanis and Angela did, and we should be able to control things better.*>

<*Right,*> Rika snorted. <*Because we* ***neeeeever*** *get stuck up shit creek without a paddle.*>

<*Good point. That's sort of been our entire existence together, hasn't it?*>

<*Yup.*>

Neither spoke for a moment, and Rika distracted herself with listening to Heather berate one of the tug pilots from Hanging Garden for nearly sending a section of the *Lance* that they believed to contain an armory down into Babylon's depths.

Garth was laughing as he listened to the exchange, but at a stern look from the captain, he turned back to his console, appearing to focus, though his shoulders were still lifting sporadically.

<*Rika?*> The word came from Piper. <*What do we do with the black hole in the ship?*>

<*Shit. How did I forget about that thing?*>

It was Niki's turn to snort. <*Seriously? It's* ***all*** *I've been thinking about.*>

<*Me too,*> Piper added. <*Well, not 'all', but you get the picture. I'm not especially keen on being on a ship that's flying around with a black hole in it.*>

<*Did we figure out how they made it so fast?*> Rika asked.

<*We did.*> Piper's tone was devoid of emotion. <*They used graviton emitters to collapse a supply of uranium into neutronium, and then hammered that down into a black hole. From there, they fed it gas from the planet to get it up to the mass they needed.*>

<*So we could dump it and then remake one if needed,*> she replied.

<*Well, sort of.*> A note of uncertainty had entered Piper's voice. <*There's not really a convenient way to just 'dump' a black hole of this mass, but it's also a pain to haul around.*>

Rika considered a few options. <*Could we kick it into the dark layer?*>

<*Sure, if you want to alter the orbits of every planet in this system,*> Piper chided. <*We either have to bleed it off, carry it around, or dump it out in interstellar space somewhere.*>

<*Which carries its own risks,*> Niki added.

<*You totally sure you don't want to get chummy with a black hole again?*> Rika asked Piper.

<*I'm really not. 'Not keen' was a nice way of saying 'fuck no'.*>

<*I guess that's that,*> Niki said. <*You know that what happened at Epsilon wasn't really your fault, right?*>

<*I enabled it all. I was blinded by ambition, and brought about my own death.*>

It was the first time that Piper had spoken about the events at Epsilon—where he'd lost the other segments of his multinodal mind—as a death.

<*You still have the data backups, right?*> Rika asked.

<You could be reconstituted if you go to Bob.>

<I would not be the same, and it would be the death of who I am now. Trust me, this is for the best. I am diminished, but I am me.>

<But you don't want to be here, on the Marauders' Lance.> Rika said the words as a statement, not a question.

<Correct. You should use this ship to its full potential. It may have been designed to shoot through stasis shields, but it would also tear through station defenses—or strike planetary targets through dense atmosphere. It's a formidable weapon. Just one I cannot operate.>

<Well, no one's asking you to operate it.> Niki's voice was conciliatory. *<Though I imagine it could happen.>*

<It ***would****,>* Piper insisted. *<You know that to be the case. Give the ship to Potter. She's patiently waited for the honor. She deserved to have the* Fury Lance.>

<What about you?> Rika asked.

A predatory note entered Piper's voice. *<Give me one of the Harriets. The ISF filled them with drones. I could wreak such destruction on the Nietzscheans with one of those ships.>*

Rika considered the AI's request. The ISF had refitted four Harriet Class carriers and brought them to the Marauders at Genevia. Each vessel was capable of housing a hundred thousand drones, though few AIs could manage such a number on their own.

Piper being amongst those few. Even without his multinodal mind, he was more powerful than any other AI Rika knew of—excepting Bob and Tangel.

<*Have you picked one out?*> Niki asked Piper.

<*Ah, you know me so well, Niki,*> he replied. <*I'd really like the* Endless Chasm. *It has a near-full loadout of drones, and the ISF outfitted it with enough automation to be run by me alone.*>

The new Harriets had all been brought in by skeleton crews of ISF personnel that had left with the rest of Carson's fleet two days ago. Rika hadn't finished her fleet re-org yet, so no new crews had moved onto the ships.

<*Very well, Captain Piper. The* Endless Chasm *is yours.*>

<*Ohhh, 'Captain'! Does that mean I'm in the Marauders now?*>

<*You will be if you take the commission,*> Rika replied.

<*A part of the Royal Space Force,*> Niki added with a laugh, then sent Rika a mental scowl. <*Don't give me that, you like the sound of it.*>

<*I suppose the whole queen thing is growing on me.*>

The AI gave a soft laugh. <*Good, because I have a little public ceremony in mind….*>

<*Oh now you're in for it.*> Piper sent a knowing wink, and Rika couldn't help but groan.

<*Stars, just do it soon so we can get it over with.*>

IN THE DARK

STELLAR DATE: 06.03.8950 (Adjusted Years)
LOCATION: *ViperTalon*, stellar dark layer
REGION: Burroughs System, Old Genevia, Nietzschean Empire

The boards lit up, flashing warnings for half the systems on the ship, but Rajiz didn't need to read them to know what happened.

<Gero! How bad's the engine?>

<I'm dumping the chamber,> the engineer replied. *<Bell got torn clear off. The reactor's about to melt through the firewall!>*

"Shit," Rajiz cursed, knowing Gero wouldn't dump a burner unless there was no other choice. *<OK, do it. Are the secondaries intact?>*

<Seem to be. I'll run tests once this thing is off the ship.>

Rajiz closed the connection, monitoring the status of the reactor on his console.

"Gonna be hard to do a corrective burn at the edge of the system when we have a missing engine," Avi said in a quiet voice.

"We're going to have to figure it out," Rajiz said, pulling up the plot.

Travel through the dark layer insystem didn't give the same speed multiplier that it did in interstellar space. Some people said it was friction, others said it was due to the star warping spacetime across multiple dimensions.

Either way, the ship's sensors showed a multiplier of just over one hundred. They'd entered the DL at a hair under 0.3*c*, which meant that they'd reach their exit point, seventy AU from the star, in nineteen minutes.

Part of his board went from red to grey, indicating that the port engine's reactor had been dumped.

<*I need test results in five,*> Avi told Gero. <*Tell me what I'm working with.*>

<*Only one set of hands down here,*> the engineer shot back. <*Oh, and Captain, can you get our muscly friends to move everything from Hold 7 to Hold 3? We need to move as much mass to the starboard side as we can.*>

<*On it.*> Rajiz sent Betty the instructions, trusting her to have no issue wrangling Jim and Jerry.

As they worked, he ran through the numbers on the burn and saw that, even with the cargo shifted, and the ship's ballast compensating, they would still have to run the starboard engine at only fifty-seven percent efficiency to maintain an even thrust.

In theory, it should be OK. The Burroughs System only had a few small planets that far out, and the Niets barely patrolled them at all.

Granted, he hadn't expected them to spend so much effort pursuing them out of the inner system, either.

"We're going to have to burn for over forty minutes in normal space to correct our vector," Avi said once she was able to run her calculations.

"Not the end of the world," Rachella spoke for the

first time in some minutes. "Will we lose a lot of speed?"

"A bit," Rajiz replied. "We'll be down close to point-three-five. Going to stretch our trip to Genevia out to almost four days."

The PLI woman pursed her lips. "Well, I suppose it can't be helped."

CAPETON COMMAND

STELLAR DATE: 06.05.8950 (Adjusted Years)
LOCATION: Capeton Command, Capeton
REGION: Genevia System, Old Genevia, Nietzschean Empire

"You know," Kora said as she and Gary stepped out of the shuttle's airlock and walked down the ramp. "I've never been up to the Triple-C before. The place is kinda…."

"Bland?" Gary asked. "Boring? Lame?"

"I was thinking…yeah, pretty much that." She gestured to scorch marks on the docking bay's bulkheads. "Plus shot up."

"Adds to the ambiance," a dockhand said as he ambled past.

Kora snorted. "When your 'splash of color' is black and grey, you need to reevaluate things."

"Can't say I disagree there," Gary said as the pair walked across the bay to the concourse that serviced smaller passenger ships.

<*OK.*> Kora turned right, following Gary toward the maglev terminal at the end of the passage. <*So our guy works maintenance in the service vessel docks, right?*>

<*Yeah, that's where we'll find him.*>

<*Well, let's not find him there,*> she said. <*He'll be ready there, have his people around him, and be in his element. We want to have our chat somewhere that he won't feel too*

comfortable.>

<*Is that really necessary? He worked with us to take Capeton Command from the Niets. He had files on who was a sympathizer and who had worked to undermine the enemy. He was an invaluable resource.*>

<*Which means he's wily,*> Kora replied. <*He's prepared, and he won't turn on anyone without some work. All the more reason to catch him off guard.*>

<*I—*> Gary stopped himself. <*OK, sorry, I'll stop complaining about this. Just don't treat him as hostile till he gives you reason, 'kay?*>

<*Deal.*> Kora gave a resolute nod. <*So, where can we find Rhon?*>

<*I just pinged him and asked if he wants to grab a drink. He's down on the docks, but suggested a bar nearby. That means he'll follow this route.*>

Gary passed Kora the two locations, with the most likely route between them highlighted. She looked over the passages Rhon would travel and noted a narrow corridor with a few service passages branching off from it.

<*Let's meet up with him there. We can head into one of those side halls and have some privacy.*>

<*Passageways,*> Gary corrected.

<*What?*>

<*In space, there are no halls. Corridors and passageways are what we have up here.*>

Kora snorted. <*That's just stupid.*>

<*I didn't say it wasn't, just what they're called.*>

She resisted an eyeroll and sent an acknowledgment as the pair hurried to the maglev, catching a train just before it left the terminal, and riding it the short distance to the service docks.

<*I hope we beat him there,*> she said as the pair strode through the corridors. <*You should have waited till we were closer to reach out.*>

<*Sorry, I'm more of a guard guy, and less of a spy guy,*> Gary countered.

<*Don't worry, after this you can go back to being guard guy,*> Kora said. <*Hopefully he'll have some good leads that will point me at a ship. Once I have that, I can crack this thing open.*>

<*You make it sound like there's definite duplicity.*>

The detective nodded. <*Nearly everyone we picked up in connection to the KK100 worked for Oda. Tremon doesn't like the mystery surrounding Arla, and neither do I.*>

Gary grunted in response, and they rode the rest of the way to the service docks in silence. On the way, Kora put in a request with the station police for access to their Link triangulation system. It confirmed that he was still routing through a node at the dock where he worked.

<*Looks like we'll beat him there,*> she said to Gary.

<*Good, we can jump out and yell 'surprise'.*>

<*I thought you were going to play along.*>

<*This* **is** *me playing along.*>

She decided not to belabor the issue with the man, and when the train reached the station, they exited with her leading the way. Four minutes later, they reached the narrow corridor, Kora confirming that Rhon had only just left.

<OK, looks like he's—>

"Gary," a voice said from behind the pair. "This doesn't seem like the way that friends would meet up. And with an unannounced guest as well."

Kora turned to see Rhon step out of an alcove, a smirk on his lips and a pulse rifle in his hands.

"Really, Rhon?" Gary asked, his eyes on the weapon. "This is how you greet a friend?"

"You're more like an acquaintance." Rhon looked past them and nodded, the gesture eliciting a sigh from Kora.

She glanced over her shoulder and saw two women and a man, all of whom were also holding rifles. "Hey, we were just looking to talk in private. We weren't looking for a shootout."

"Well, we've never been known to turn one down," Rhon said as his people searched and disarmed them. Once satisfied they were secure, he gave a curt nod. "OK, that's not true, but you get the picture. Let's move."

"Where are we going?" Kora asked, while sending a message to Gary. *<Go with it, let's see what we learn.>*

<And what if we learn how to be dead?>

<Then Rika will kill this asshole. I'm transmitting our location to a team of Marauders no one knows is on the station.>

"Don't think that you can tell the cops where you

are," Rhon said. "I have them in my pocket. No one's going to know where you are till I'm satisfied that you're on the right side."

"Which side is that?" Kora asked. "I'm new to this whole spy thing. I could use some pointers. Like…is it the side that just liberated us from our occupiers, or is it someone else? Did they do something to free me from oppression? I'd like to thank them if they did."

Rhon only shook his head, and gestured for Kora and Gary to keep walking.

They passed through a variety of narrow service corridors, leading ever deeper into rarely visited sections of station where rust and grime hinted at an older, and much less pristine, history for the place. Eventually they came to a pumping station that didn't appear to have pumped anything in decades, and Rhon gestured for Kora and Gary to stand in front of a large pipe that rested on the deck.

"This is stupid, Rhon," Gary said. "We're all on the same side, we just want some intel."

"Any reason you were going to ambush me?" Rhon asked, sharing a knowing look with his three compatriots.

"Oh, I don't know," Kora tapped a finger against her chin. "Maybe the way people keep trying to kill Rika…oh, and me by extension, since a nuke going off in Jague would have ended my time in the 'verse a bit early as well."

"A lot of things are unsettled." Rhon nodded, his

expression softening. "But you're not exactly on the 'trust without question' list, Gary. You were working with Weick, and he sided with the Niets. And you're a total unknown, Kora."

"You can look me up," she said with a shrug, watching Rhon's hands as the man interlaced his fingers and then separated them over and over.

It was a self-soothing sign, which meant he was agitated, but that didn't point to any particular action or guilt.

The man nodded. "I have. You have a good record, though I've come to learn that cops are easy to buy—at least after they've worked for the Niets for years. So who owns you, Detective Kora?"

"I've been assigned by Chancellor Tremon to find out how the KK100 ended up on Belgium," Kora said. "We know who had it, but we're not entirely certain how it got there. I want to trace its provenance and find out if there are others seeking to do Rika and her Marauders any harm."

"So you're investigating the resistance?" one of the other captors asked, but Rhon held up a hand and shook his head.

Kora shrugged. "I'm following leads. If they take me to the resistance, then that's who I'll investigate. If they take me to Nietzschean sympathizers, then I follow to that end."

"Sounds like a witch hunt," Rhon muttered.

"It's only a witch hunt if there's no real crime," she

replied. "Twice now, KK100s have been used in an attempt to subvert the mechs. That's evidence of a crime."

"Under whose law?" Rhon asked.

"New Genevia signed on to the Scipio Alliance." Kora folded her arms across her chest. "As such, we've adopted Section 2 of the Phobos Accords. There's a lot in there about the sanctity of personhood. Stuff that a KK100—stars, pretty much the entire mech program—violates."

Rhon snorted and shook his head. "So the first thing we do after getting out from one oppressor is sign on as a vassal of another state? From what I hear, the Scipians aren't much better than the Niets. Did you know they have a place called the 'Hall of Heroes' that is constructed from the bones of their enemies?"

Kora shook her head, fixing Rhon with an unblinking stare. "I'm not here to debate the morality of Scipio, who we're *not* a vassal state of, by the way. They had to sign on to the Phobos Accords too. What I *am* here to find out is who could have brought Arla into the Genevia System, and did they bring the KK100 with her?"

"Nothing heavy, then." Rhon coughed out a laugh.

"Seriously?" Gary shook his head, disgust etched into his features. "Are you actually protecting Arla? She tried to kill Rika, and may have given a KK100 to the Niets! She's not aligned with the resistance—stars, there *is* no need for a resistance anymore."

"Maybe, maybe not." Rhon pursed his lips for a

moment before continuing. "It's one thing to be freed by a bunch of mechs—that's what they're for: kicking ass. But to be ruled by one of those freaks? I'm sorry, but that just doesn't sit right with me."

The other captors shook their heads in agreement with Rhon, their expressions hardening, an unspoken challenge for Kora and Gary to either agree with their sentiment or face some unpleasant consequences.

"You're such fucking idiots," Kora muttered. "You're even dumber than Oda. At least he was just a blind fool hiding in a cave. You've been out here in the world. You've seen what it was like under the Niets. Most of us were indentured servants at best, slaves at worst. Rika and her Marauders *freed* us, and all you can do is see a machine, not the woman."

"And you've been blinded by a false liberation," Rhon shot back. "The mechs are insane, all of them. That's why we had Discipline in the war. To make sure they didn't kill us all."

"No," Gary ground out the word. "We used Discipline because the mechs were neither volunteers nor criminals. We picked up kids off the street, *kids*, and turned them into killing machines. So yeah, guess what, we had to beat them into submission. But you know what? They don't want payback, they just want to be accepted by their own people—they want it so much, they put their lives on the line time and time again to save us."

"That's just what they want you to think," Rhon

muttered.

"Stars, this has gone on long enough," Kora said, shaking her head in disgust. "You're just too blind to see what's really going on."

"Oh, I don't think I'm blind at all," Rhon shot back, his eyes narrowing as he took a step toward her. "You're the one who's sucking on the end of Rika's gun-arm."

Kora nodded. "OK, fine. If that's how you see it, then we'll have to do this a different way."

"What are you—"

Rhon's words were cut off as five mechs appeared, two in front of the would-be captors, and three behind.

"I really hate ingratitude," Lieutenant Crudge said as he slapped the rifle out of Rhon's hands. "*Especially* when it comes from people who should be close allies."

A sneer settled on Rhon's lips as he gazed up at the AM-4. "So is this where you show us your true colors?"

Crudge shook his head. "Oh heck no. I was just walking by when I heard a ruckus. You're in Detective Kora's custody."

Kora let out an evil chuckle and cracked her knuckles. "See, Rhon, these mechs are actually pretty decent folk. Most of them were either asleep or out with civilized people beyond Nietzschea for the past few years. Me on the other hand, well, I was a cop in occupied territory. I learned a lot of interesting techniques to get the information I need. You ready to get acquainted with them?"

*****

Kora settled into her chair across from Rhon, leaning back and taking in the man before her. He still looked as haughty as before, but had folded his arms across his chest, hands wrapped around his sides.

It was another self-soothing gesture, a giveaway that he was feeling out of sorts, vulnerable, and that he had something to hide—not that Kora was surprised.

The silence between them stretched on for a minute, then five, then ten. Finally, as they crossed the twelve-minute mark, Rhon spoke up.

"If I wanted the silent treatment, I could have just told my wife her ass is too big."

"Ohhh!" Kora gasped. "What a burn! That's it, you're out of my league, there's no way I'll get anything out of you."

For a moment, the man's eyes widened in surprise, a look of victory flashing across his face only to be replaced by suspicion. "You think you're funny, don't you?"

"I'm a pretty humorous person," Kora nodded in agreement, a genuine smile on her lips. "I know how to get the yuk-yuks."

"Yeah, well, don't quit your day job."

"Oh I don't need to. See, I torture people like you with my terrible jokes during interrogations, and then sell the videos. It's a double whammy. I get paid twice for working once."

Rhon frowned. "Isn't that…illegal?"

"Is it?" Kora tilted her head, adopting a confused look. "To be honest, the law has been so fluid lately, it's hard to tell what's legal and what's not. I suppose it might be immoral. I bet you know alllll about doing immoral things to achieve your ends, don't you, Rhon, ol' buddy boy?"

"Don't think you can equate what I do for the resistance with what you do for your Nietzschean and mech masters."

"Well, if I'm doing it all for a pocket full of credits, then I'm doing it for myself, aren't I?"

"Whatever. You're not going to do anything now. I bet those mechs are watching."

Kora nodded vigorously. "I really hope they are. They've seen some serious shit, I'm hoping that afterward they'll give me pointers. I mean, what I've always wondered is whether or not it's better to start with the fingers or toes."

"Nice try," Rhon snorted. "Have at it. I'll just get new ones later."

"Rhon, Rhon, Rhon." Kora shook her head. "You don't get it. There *is* no later for you. Well, I mean, we'll hold onto you long enough to ensure that your intel checks out, then off with your head!"

"You really like to ham it up, don't you?"

A wicked grin settled on Kora's lips, and she flicked a hand to her left, showing footage of a darkened city street. The sound of weapons fire echoed between the buildings, flashes of light illuminating blown-out storefronts and half-burned ground cars.

"This is Denmar in the Parsons System, back around midway through the war," Kora explained. "It's some vid I managed to get from a Nietzschean archive."

"OK, so what? We were all in the war, we all saw shit."

"I saw some shit." Kora nodded. "But I was too young to be in the GAF, and lucky enough not to see any major combat—not like this, at least."

The weapons fire grew louder, and then the shadowy figures of SMI-2 mechs came into view, moving down the street, firing at unseen enemies.

One of the mechs took rocket fire, and while one helped their fallen comrade, the third mech cast about for the enemy—who had just stepped in front of the groundcar in the foreground.

"This is where it gets good," Kora whispered.

The mech charged the Nietzschean soldier and slammed him into the ground. Her clawed feet latched onto his chest and she reached down with her three-fingered left hand and grabbed his helmet.

A blood-curdling shriek filled the air, a combination of screams and rending metal. A moment later, the mech was holding a helmet with pieces of reinforced spinal column hanging down in a ragged, blood-soaked ruin.

"Look at that," Kora whispered gleefully. "Isn't that amazing?"

Rhon shot her a look that was half terror, half fury.

"Why the fuck are you showing me this?"

"Well, that's our new magnus," she said, smiling sweetly. "That's Rika on one of her early missions. Stars, I look up to her so much. I'm going to get a powered armor suit and try that move out on your pals to get it right for your turn."

The man across from her had visibly paled, his eyes darting between Kora and the frozen image of Rika holding her gruesome trophy aloft.

"You're serious…."

"Well, here's how I look at it." She leant forward, elbows on her knees. "Rika likes to win. A lot. Which is good, because she *does* win. But don't for a minute think that she's all about honor and the clean kill. Rumor has it that she's beaten people to death with their own arms. So imagine how she must feel about people smuggling a couple of KK100s into the system with the intent of taking control of her mechs and enslaving them again. Not only that, but whoever did it worked with the Niets, and got her favorite ship blown up."

Rhon pursed his lips as she spoke, his jaw tightening, fingers gripping his sides.

"So do you really think she's going to be too upset with me if I do what I have to with you? Unless…" Kora sat back and crossed her legs, "you tell me what I need to know without any muss and fuss. Then I bet we can work out some sort of deal that doesn't see what's left of you being slopped into a bucket."

For a moment, it looked like the man was going to

double down in his denial, but then he glanced at the cameras in the corners, knowing all too well that someone was watching and hadn't seen fit to stop Kora yet.

"The mechs," she whispered. "They're pretty pissed about someone trying to mindfuck them. The lieutenant is cheering in my ear, he's even picking out the best exo-armor to do the spine pulling bit. I—"

"OK!" Rhon shouted. "OK...please, look, I'm just doing my part here. I didn't bring in Arla *or* the KK100, but I know who did."

"Spill it," Kora hissed, her eyes narrowed to slits. "No more fucking around."

"Captain Belfas. He skippers the *Jay Rig*."

"Which is where?" Kora asked.

Rhon closed his eyes and heaved a sigh. "It's here at Capeton Command. He's fueling up before heading back to Burroughs."

"What for?" Kora pressed. "Why go back there?"

"I don't know. He said something about getting someone to finish the job."

AN UNWELCOME MESSAGE

STELLAR DATE: 06.05.8950 (Adjusted Years)
LOCATION: NMS *Kraska*, approaching Valhalla
REGION: Capitol, Pruzia System, Nietzschean Empire

Admiral Hammond reread one of the speeches he planned to give to the High Council for what had to be the tenth time. There were two variants; the first was to be used if the *Pinnacle* and its tech was secured, and the second if it was not.

If anyone could capture the ship at this stage, it would be Doctor Xa. Even so, Hammond was a realist. Xa was up against Rika, and thus far, she'd bested Nietzschea at every turn. The speech he'd give in the event the spy failed was the one he was spending the most time on.

"No," he muttered, reconsidering a particular turn of phrase that did not paint Constantine's decisions in a good light. "Or maybe yes."

The admiral rose and strode around to the front of his desk, stopping before it and stretching out his arms. He still hadn't decided if he would appeal to the council to back him, or tear them down and support Admiral Yara.

Initial reports of the emperor's death had been sent as soon as he'd jumped from Genevia to Pruzia. Over the following few hours, everyone of any importance, from Lord Poulos of the High Council to naval quartermasters inquiring about refit plans for the counterstrike, had contacted Hammond.

Both Poulos and Yara had made it abundantly clear that he stood no chance of taking control of the empire on his own. What interested Hammond the most was how strident they'd both been. Rather than certainty in their own power, the admiral and high councilor's insistence that he needed to side with them—against the other, of course—smacked of desperation. Still, that didn't mean he could stake a claim on his own.

But perhaps he could ride in the wake of one of the leaders until the time was right—

<*Message drone has just jumped in,*> his chief aide, Major Fennel, announced. <*It looks like Xa failed to secure the* Pinnacle. *Reports are that Rika has captured him.*>

<*He'll never talk,*> Hammond said, as much to reassure himself as anything else. The spy was loyal, and would commit suicide before betraying the empire. *Unless there's some angle he could play….*

<*Three systems have begun the scorched-earth retreats. We should see a response from the Marauders soon.*>

<*Good. And the strike forces?*>

<*All ready. We'll hit them coming and going, sir.*>

Hammond nodded, though no one could see it. <*Damn straight we will.*>

While capturing the *Pinnacle* would have earned him a lot of respect, killing Rika and dispersing her Marauders would gain him even more.

"And who knows," he said aloud while stretching

once more. “Maybe then I can waltz back into Genevia and just take the *Pinnacle*.”

HOMECOMING

STELLAR DATE: 06.07.8950 (Adjusted Years)
LOCATION: Mount Genevia, Belgium
REGION: Genevia System, New Genevian Alliance

"I can't tell if it feels good to be planetside, or if I'm excited for the big event in a few days," Chase said as he walked alongside Rika in the mountaintop estate.

She rolled her shoulders and glanced around at what once had been the Genevian presidential residence, but was now being referred to as the Royal Palace on the feeds.

"It's a mixed bag for me. I don't mind being downworld, but this place…some mixed emotions here."

"It's optics." Chase placed a hand on her shoulder. "The people need to see us taking our sovereignty back from the Niets. No better way to do that than to re-establish our rule here."

"Sure." Rika nodded. "I get that. I think I just miss the *Fury Lance.* That ship was home, not this drafty place."

"I don't think it's actually drafty."

"Feels drafty," Rika groused. "Stars, what am I talking about? I don't have skin. Who cares if there's a draft."

"I wasn't gonna mention that, but…."

"Har har."

The pair reached the end of the hall, and the doors

swung open, admitting them to what Rika privately thought of as the throne room—largely because it was where Emperor Constantine had met with her while sitting on a throne.

At present, a large, round table sat in the middle of the room with over twenty chairs situated around it. Half of them were filled with her Marauders, while the other half were occupied by civilians, some of whom she'd only met over the Link.

This is my government.

The assemblage rose as one as she entered the room, and waited until she settled into her chair before returning to their seats.

On her left sat Tremon and six others who headed up the civilian leadership, while on her right were Chase and the company commanders and senior ship captains of the Marauders.

She felt the notable absence of Colonel Borden of the ISF. He'd been an unshakable presence since Tangel had charged Rika with taking down Nietzschea. But with New Canaan under attack, he'd returned to the ISF's home system, along with Admiral Carson.

"Nine months ago, we chased the fleeing remnants of a Nietzschean armada to the Sepe system," Rika began, her gaze sweeping across the faces of those assembled. "My Marauders were newly formed, only a few weeks out of our first battle in the Hercules System, and fresh from the fight in Albany. Tangel, Field Marshal of the Scipio Alliance, had hired the Marauders to do the impossible: take back Genevia and defeat the Nietzscheans. Even she expected it to take the better part of a decade."

She paused, a smile flitting across her lips as she considered the events since leaving Albany.

"Let's just say that we're a bit ahead of schedule."

Muted laughter came from those present. The mechs and ship commanders all wore expressions of proud satisfaction, while the civilians appeared somewhat uncertain, but appreciative.

"Exactly what we do from here is what we're here to discuss today," Rika said. "Captain Travis's battlegroup has already jumped out to Gerra. We'll likely not know for a few more days how things are shaping up there, but we have to assume that the Niets will be doing the same thing in other nearby systems."

"What if they're retreating from all Genevian systems, burning as they go?"

The question came from Regan Harl, the newly minted minister of finance. Rika couldn't tell if he was genuinely worried or being combative, but Barne responded before she had a chance to consider it further.

"Well, aside from the fact that it will take a year for retreat orders to filter across Old Genevia, there's no reason for them to fall back yet. They want to create a crisis that we have to respond to here around the Genevia System."

"Be a mighty big crisis if they burn every system in Old Genevia," Commissioner Megan of the Genevia

Federal Police said.

"And it would unite us against them once more," Rika said. "Which is why they won't do it. Nietzscheans are opportunists. They'll milk everything they can out of Old Genevia before they turn and run."

"So what is your plan, Magnus?" Leslie asked with a twinkle in her eye.

<*You wanted to say 'my queen', didn't you?*> Rika asked.

Leslie sent a wink over the Link. <*Maybe.*>

"We're still in the midst of fleet re-org," she replied aloud. "But in two days, we'll be ready to send aid to Burroughs, Oran, and Morres. Ten ships each, which will leave a Marauder fleet consisting of seventy-three ships in this system."

"Stars, that's not a lot to defend an entire system," Commissioner Megan said in a quiet voice.

"You're right," Rika replied with a resolute nod. "It's not. However, if the Niets do hit us, they're going to do it in the outer system, most likely at Orden Station, out by where the jump gates were set up."

"Were?" Regan Harl asked. "I hadn't heard that they'd moved."

"And you won't," Rika replied. "At least, not outside this room. The gates are all coming insystem, but we constructed decoys, a little bait to lure the Niets in."

"What if the Niets have more jump gates?" Tremon asked, an eyebrow raised. "I know it's unlikely, but it's possible."

"It is," Rika replied with a nod. "However, the Niets

won't know that the ISF has left—at least not yet. They won't strike where they expect the bulk of Carson's fleet to be. That means they won't jump deep insystem. That would see them facing a three-day flight to the closest jump point."

"Let's just say they have a bunch of suicidal commanders," Regan Harl pressed. "Are we going to leave Belgium undefended?"

Rika shook her head. "No, I have a plan to keep Belgium safe, don't worry."

From there, the conversation moved to appropriations measures aimed both at bolstering government resources, and also at securing assets that the Nietzscheans had seized and redistributed to their own lackeys. Rika wished they didn't have to waste time on such mundane tasks, but Tremon had impressed on her the importance of showing the populace that she cared about justice.

Four hours later, the meeting was finally wrapping up when Chief Ona called down from the *Marauders' Lance*.

<Magnus Rika, we've just picked up a distress call. A ship from the Burroughs System is talking about the Niets getting ready to raze Chad.>

<Getting ready?> Rika asked.

<That's what they're saying. Piping it through to you.>

Rika accepted the message, and a lanky man appeared in her mind.

<This is Captain Rajiz of the ViperTalon. *We've just*

boosted away from Chad, where the Niets are prepping Razers. From what we can tell, they don't have enough yet to make a huge mess, but they're sending more in and pulling their troops off-world. You've probably got bigger fish to fry—>

The captain's voice cut out, and he glanced to his left.

<*You want to give it? Fine. Have at it.*>

He stepped back, and a woman walked into view. She was rail thin with a pinched face, but her eyes were wide and expressive.

<*Please, Colonel Rika,*> she began. <*We've heard about how you saved Blue Ridge and Iberia. The people on Chad have been through enough already, don't let the Niets cut them down just to make a statement. Let this be a great start for New Genevia, a start where we help one another and force the Niets back.*>

The captain cleared his throat, shaking his head at the woman before speaking once more to Rika. <*We're passing along the latest charts of the Burroughs System, plus vid from what we saw them preparing. Let us know if you're able to help.*>

The message ended, and Rika pursed her lips. <*Thanks, Ona. Send them an acknowledgment message.*>

<*Yes, ma'am.*>

None of the senior leadership had left the room yet, and Rika rose and leant against the table. "We've got a new development. It looks like the Niets are still preparing to hit Chad. If we send a force now, we can stop them."

"Chad?" Regan Harl asked. "Of all the places."

"It's a place with our people on it," Rika replied. "We're going to defend it with extreme prejudice, show the Niets how we feel about them trashing our worlds."

"We have thirty ships here at Belgium," Chase said. "Which should we send?"

Rika's gaze met Heather's. "We're sending the *Marauders' Lance* and a destroyer escort. Captain, show the Niets what payback looks like."

The SMI barked a laugh and rubbed her hands. "Oh with pleasure. Who're my ground pounders gonna be?"

"Colonel Chase?" Rika quirked a smile at the method of informing Chase of his promotion. "Who would you like to send from your battalion?"

He cocked an eyebrow and then winked at her. "Well, if we're sending the *Marauders' Lance,* then it's gonna be M Company. I'll make sure Captain Karen is ready to roll."

"Oh hell yeah." Heather barked a laugh and slapped Chase on the back. "You and I are gonna have a hell of a time."

"Chase is staying here," Rika said. "You're in command this time, Colonel Heather."

"Oh ho! Colonel?" the SMI cackled. "Stars, today just keeps getting better and better."

Rika rolled her eyes and laughed at the giddy mech. "Get out of here and make sure your ship is ready to go. Last I heard, Bondo was still working on getting the stasis shields calibrated."

"Oh we'll be ready." Heather was already striding

across the room and called back over her shoulder, "Trust me, the Niets are gonna wish they'd never fucked with Chad."

A moment later, she was out of the room, and Barne shook his head, laughing quietly. "You know she's from Chad, right?"

Rika gave the general a smile and winked. "You don't say?"

INSYSTEM

STELLAR DATE: 06.08.8950 (Adjusted Years)
LOCATION: *ViperTalon*, approaching Babylon
REGION: Genevia System, New Genevian Alliance

"I thought you wanted to get back to Burroughs and aid in the defense of Chad," Rajiz said as he settled into a chair in the galley, eyeing Rachella over the rim of his coffee cup.

"I did." She nodded while buttering her toast at the counter. "But that was when I wasn't sure if the Marauders would send aid. With their jump gates, they'll have been there for over a week by the time we brake and boost back out on a vector for Burroughs."

"Sure." Rajiz shrugged. "Isn't it your home, though? Chad?"

"No," Rachella shook her head. "I'm actually from Genevia, on Shaya. The PLI has me working all over, and since I'm here, I need to check on a few things."

"Wait a second," Rajiz set his cup down. "I thought that the PLI is just a front for the resistance. If that's the case, why do you need to run ops here? There's nothing to resist."

Rachella regarded him silently for a moment and then took a bite of her toast, chewing thoughtfully before answering.

"Well, the Marauders are mercs, and from what I

hear, they've signed Genevia on to some sort of galactic war. They might need some resisting as well."

"I highly doubt that the war is galactic," Rajiz replied. "Humanity is barely past the edges of the Orion Arm."

"You need to read the fine print, Captain." She grabbed her plate and glass of orange juice, joining him at the table. "According to this Scipio Alliance we've bound ourselves to, humanity is in the Sagittarius and Perseus Arms as well."

"Oh?" Rajiz frowned. "I must have glossed over that part. I mean, you're right, it seems like a pretty big conflict, but that doesn't really matter."

"It doesn't?" Rachella appeared genuinely surprised.

"No, not really. I'm told that Magnus Rika has her mandate to secure Genevia and take down Nietzschea. However, from the feeds I was reading, that's been the Marauder's plan all along, so this is more like an alliance of convenience—one that has kitted out their ships pretty nicely, I might add."

"Still doesn't mean they're altruistic," Rachella countered. "You'd do well to remember that. There was a reason we kept mechs on a short leash during the war."

"A K1R once saved my entire platoon," Rajiz replied with a languid shrug.

He wondered if Rachella and her two guards might have planned to stay in the Genevia System all alone. *What is their ulterior motive?*

"Sure, mechs saved a lot of us. But they were under

orders and Discipline."

"These mechs aren't, and they're doing pretty damn well. Makes me think we might have done things backwards during the war."

Rachella snorted. "Don't be ridiculous."

"Ridiculous?" Rajiz leant forward. "We lost the war. Saying we shouldn't have done things differently is ludicrous. Especially when these Marauders are stomping on the Niets over and over."

"I don't trust their stated reasoning, sorry," she said in a tone that brooked no argument.

Rajiz rose and downed the rest of his coffee. "Yeah, well, I don't trust yours. When we get to Hanging Gardens Station, you're off my ship. Got it?"

For a moment, he thought that Rachella was going to fight him on the decision, but then she nodded.

"Yeah. Fine."

BECKY'S BAD DAY

STELLAR DATE: 06.08.8950 (Adjusted Years)
LOCATION: Hanging Gardens Station, Babylon
REGION: Genevia System, New Genevian Alliance

Becky stood on the station's plas deck, a scowl etched into her delicate features as she watched the service crew connect fuel lines to her ship.

"Manual hookups," she muttered. "Stars, where am I? The asscrack of nowhere?"

"The station's all backed up after the fighting nearby," Dara said from her side. "I know it's weird to be down on commercial docks, but once we get fueled up, we'll be gone."

The captain of the *Slyfe* nodded absently as she tried to come up with what could be a safer harbor than Genevia. A modicum of worry for what her wife might be facing in the Parsons System flitted about in the back of her mind, but Becky knew that Geni could handle pretty much anything—especially with her corporate fleet to protect herself.

"*I'm* the one out here in danger," she whispered.

"Pardon?" Dara asked. "What danger?"

"What danger?" Becky squeaked. "There's danger all around us! We're in danger central. Any one of these people passing by us could be unsavory criminals, ready to rob us or worse."

"I do tend to like unsavory types," Dara said with a soft sigh. "Too bad we never get to spend much time with them."

"You need to stop thinking with your clam." Becky threw a disapproving glance at Dara. "I don't think we should leave the Genevia System, but I don't want to stay here. We should get to Belgium. I hear there are going to be some state parties. I bet we could get into them."

"Becky." Dara's tone was filled with disapproval. "There's a war going on, how can you think of parties?"

"*State* parties," she corrected. "Trust me, those are going to be the safest places in the system. We just need to get there and get on the list."

"How do you propose to do that?"

"Why, Dara!" Becky placed a hand on her chest. "The same way I do everything. I unleash my charm."

"So that's what we're calling it now?"

*****

Kora stepped off the transport with Gary at her side. The pair shared a look as they turned to the right and began walking through the passenger terminal.

<*I've confirmed that the* Jay Rig *has docked,*> Kora said, watching the people as they moved along the concourse.

The last few weeks had been surreal, seeing the Nietzscheans defeated and New Genevia established under Rika. What was even stranger, however, was that life just seemed to go on for most people, with almost no real change.

Except there was a change. Somehow, the atmosphere seemed lighter than it had the last time she'd been through Hanging Gardens. The crowds were more vocal, people smiling at one another and small groups forming to chat.

<*Everyone seems excited about the coronation,*> Gary commented, apparently on the same train of thought. <*I didn't leave the Refuge much during the occupation, but it's sure nice to just be out and about, not having to worry about Niets arresting me.*>

<*Except that we've just traded one worry for another,*> Kora replied.

<*Yeah…but I wouldn't object to scrounging up a moment to breathe. Instead, we're worried that some group of asshats is going to ruin the freedom we just got.*>

<*Funny how that works. I wonder if we're all so used to being stressed about the Niets that we're just finding something new to latch onto.*>

Gary shrugged, smiling at a group who was handing out flowers, but declining to take one. <*Could be. I know it's going to take me some time to figure out what normal even is, let alone settle into it. I feel bad leaving my 'toon back on Belgium as well.*>

<*Not the sort of op we can do with a whole troop of soldiers following us around. Though I do miss the mechs we left behind on Capeton. Having invisible warriors at your beck and call sure is nice.*>

<You can say that again.> Gary cleared his throat. *<So, any clues as to why Captain Belfas flew* **here** *when Rhon said he was going to Burroughs?>*

<Nothing that stands out yet,> Kora replied. *<I mean, he must have needed to get something or someone, right?>*

The pair reached the maglev terminal and boarded a train bound for the commercial docks, where the *Jay Rig* was berthed.

<Has he filed anything about his next destination?>

<No, not yet.> Kora was tempted to give Gary direct access to the police databases she was accessing, but worried that might tip their hand. Her requests for access were less likely to trigger any alerts, given the new rules for system-wide cooperation between police departments.

<Gotta be something, maybe a ship inbound from Burroughs, or someone else going there that he's grouping up with? With the Marauders fighting Niets there, it might make sense to go in with a convoy.>

Kora considered that, flipping through the STC's logs until something jumped out.

<Well, shit,> she whispered.

<Oh?>

<That ship, the one that came in with the message about the Niets getting ready to hit Chad. It just docked here an hour ago.>

Gary let out a low whistle. *<That seems rather coincidental. Which is to say, not that coincidental at all.>*

<Kinda feeling the same way.>

The train pulled away from the station and began to pick up speed as it followed the curve of the docking ring, shifting laterally across the great wheel to the commercial docks.

<*What do you say we go pay the* ViperTalon *a visit,*> Kora suggested. <*I think that might be a better start than hitting up the* Jay Rig.>

<*You're the detective,*> Gary replied with a laugh. <*I'm just your muscle at this point.*>

<*Don't sell yourself short.*> Kora winked. <*You could also be my 'in' if they're resistance…or my bait.*>

<*Oh joy.*>

* * * * *

Rajiz watched as Rachella and her two goons—who he'd grown to like over the past few days—got ready to depart from the ship.

Something had changed in the woman's demeanor in the prior hour. She'd sent and received a few messages, and after each one, her smile had faded a little more. Now her brow was furrowed with a deep scowl, and she seemed to be snapping at Jim and Jerry more than usual.

Initially, the plan had been for her to refuel and then return to Burroughs, but that had also changed. She hadn't said what her next stop was, but Rajiz didn't really care that much. Not having to make a trip back to Chad—especially with the Niets and Marauders fighting in the system—was a gift he wasn't going to question.

She glanced back at him where he stood in the corridor with Avi at his side.

"So where are you going next?" she asked, echoing his thoughts.

"Well, I still have to deliver that little knickknack we picked up from the Niets on Chad," he replied. "That'll square me away with Kershaw, and then when things have calmed down, I'll pass back through Burroughs to get what the PLI owes me."

She cocked an eyebrow. "The way we left it, you kind of work for the PLI now."

Rajiz snorted. "I only agreed to that nonsense to get out of the system—and maybe I had a bit of bleedingheartitis for all those poor schleps on Chad. But let's be perfectly clear, Rachella, the *ViperTalon* is certainly open for contracts, but no one owns her but me."

The PLI woman rolled her eyes and shrugged. "Fine. Have it your way. Working for my people could have opened a lot of doors."

"You know what I think?" Rajiz asked, taking a step closer to her. "I think that the PLI got too used to the criminal enterprise aspects of their resistance, and a bit too cavalier about how much the lives of the people really mattered."

"Oh?" She lifted a doubting brow. "And you're a man of the people?"

"Fuck no." Rajiz shook his head. "I don't pretend to be anything I'm not."

They stared at one another for a few seconds, and then the light above the airlock turned green, signaling that the ship had matched station pressure.

"Thanks for the ride, Captain." Then she was gone.

"Good riddance," Avi muttered. "I never liked her."

"You never like anyone," Rajiz muttered as he turned and walked up the corridor.

"Not true," she called after. "I like you."

Rajiz had just made it to the ladder when Gero messaged him.

<*Someone's at the airlock requesting a chat with the captain.*>

<*Seriously? It's not Rachella, is it?*>

Gero snorted. <*If it was her, I'd have said her name, not 'someone'.*>

<*Well does this 'someone' have a name?*>

<*No,*> the engineer replied. <*But I think she's a cop.*>

<*Oh? What makes you think that?*>

<*Well, she's got that look. Plus, the guy standing with her is clearly a soldier. He even has the haircut.*>

Rajiz groaned and turned back, nearly running into Avi. "Stars, woman, what are you doing following me?"

"Uh…going back up to the bridge? I want to start the preflight early so that as soon as the station's topped us off, we can get out of here. I don't like being this close to Babylon."

The captain chuckled. "Is it those old spacer stories about there being dragons in the clouds?"

"No," she blushed, shaking her head. "Just too close

to where the fighting's been lately."

"Sure," Rajiz winked at her as he walked past and returned to the airlock.

Once there, he saw a tall woman who did have a bit of the 'cocksure cop' look, and a man who Gero had correctly pegged as a soldier.

<*She could be corporate,*> he said to the engineer. <*And he could be ex-military security.*>

<*Wanna put credit down on it?*> the engineer asked with a greedy laugh.

The captain didn't reply, instead extending his hand to the woman as he walked through the airlock. "Captain Rajiz, I'm told you'd like to speak to me?"

"Kora," she shook his hand. "This is Gary. This is the sort of chat that we'd rather go in for."

"In?" he asked, cocking an eyebrow. "Do you mean 'aboard'?"

"Sure," she nodded. "That."

Something about her said that she wasn't the woman to split hairs with over spacer terms, and he nodded, stepping back and gesturing for her to enter the ship.

Once they were around the corner, the woman stopped and folded her arms across her chest. "OK, Captain. Spill it. What are you really doing here?"

HELL HATH NO FURY

STELLAR DATE: 06.08.8950 (Adjusted Years)
LOCATION: GMS *Marauders' Lance,* Chad
REGION: Burroughs System, New Genevian Alliance

<*Bondo, give me the good news.*>

Heather drummed her fingers impatiently on the arm of her command chair, still getting used to the cavernous bridge aboard the *Marauders' Lance*—which she still privately thought of as the *The Even More Furious Lance.*

Despite her desire to be underway in an hour, Bondo had informed her that the *Lance* still didn't have its jump mirror recalibrated after plowing through Babylon's clouds.

What followed was four hours of sitting in front of the Belgium jump gate array, waiting for the engineer to proclaim himself satisfied with the mirror's alignment.

<*You know you can't rush this shit, right?*> Bondo snapped, clearly agitated by her frequent status requests.

<*Right what?*> Heather asked.

<*What?*> Bondo's mental tone sounded distracted.

<*Cooooooolonel.*>

<*Stars, woman. Yay, you got promoted. I'm so happy for you.*>

Heather sent the lieutenant a mental image of her foot kicking him in the ass. <*So are you done?*>

<*Not if you're threatening violence.*>

<Lieutenant Carson….>

The engineer sent a tired laugh and then a feeling of acknowledgment. *<Yeah. We're good to jump. Stripes is still working on that last stasis shield generator, so give us at least half an hour before we get shot at after jumping.>*

Heather snorted. *<Sure, I'll let any Niets we see know that we need a timeout until we're ready.>*

<Good, make sure you patch me into that comm. Of course, you could also just pretend to be a Nietzschean commander. This **is** *one of their ships.>*

<I've got hives just thinking about doing that.>

The engineer barked a laugh. *<You realize you don't have skin, right?>*

<They're internal.>

<You should see a medic about that.>

Heather didn't reply to the lieutenant, and instead addressed Chief Garth. "The old man in the ass-end of our glorious new ship tells me we're good to go."

"Isn't he in the bow, Colonel?" Garth asked. "I mean, that's where the mirror is."

"Whatever, it sounded better that way," she replied. "Get us lined up. Chief Ona, let the gate control know that we're ready to jump

"Yes ma'am!" Ona's tone was chipper, and she set to her task. "I can't wait for the Niets to lose their shit when they realize this ship isn't on their side."

<I have to admit, that's going to be fun,> Potter said. *<Too bad we won't be able to see their faces.>*

"Look at you, Potter," Heather laughed. "All

vindictive."

<*Nerves,*> the AI replied. <*Well, my version of nerves. This is a* ***really*** *big ship. Honestly, I have no idea how the Niets planned to run the thing without an AI.*>

"People," Garth muttered. "Lots and lots of people."

"Well, there are exactly eleven of us," Heather said. "We'll have to make do."

Ona nodded. "Really, though, it's not as though the Niets will have sent their best and brightest to Burroughs."

"Ouch!" Heather exclaimed. "That smarts."

"Gate Control acknowledges," Ona said a moment later, her voice assuming a formal tone. "They're firing it up."

On the forward display, the largest of the jump gates sparked to life, its antimatter-powered emitters releasing exotic energy that the mirrors focused into a whirling ball of not-space.

Heather always found the visual mesmerizing—and also tried to remind herself that she wasn't looking at a black hole that could swallow the ship in an instant. Trying not to think of *that* reminded her of the small black hole within the *Lance.*

From what she knew, it was possible to take a DMG ship through a jump gate, even though logic said that slinging one black hole past another was not a wise decision.

"Take us in," she directed Garth, forcing herself not to think of it any further.

"Aye, ma'am."

The ship eased forward toward the gate, the chief finessing the vector to ensure they were directly aligned with a position one light second behind Chad's orbit. The forward display showed a countdown, and when it hit zero, the ship's mirror touched the ball of energy, removing the *Marauders' Lance* from normal spacetime and hurtling them light years distant.

Less than a second later, normal space snapped back into place around them, the forward display showing the planet Chad, and a smattering of ships moving around the world.

"OK, let's—" Heather's words were cut off by half the consoles on the bridge flashing critical warnings. An alarm began to blare, and she rose from her seat. "Potter, what's going on?"

<*It's our black hole! It's come unmoored!*>

"Unmoored?" the colonel exclaimed. "How is that even possible?"

<*Well, I guess it didn't like kissing the event horizon of the gate's black hole. It's still within the chamber, just don't change vector—at all!*>

"You hear that, Garth?"

"Fuck, yeah," the chief nodded from his station. "Steady as she goes. Not going to waver a hair."

<*It's the grav emitters in the chamber,*> Bondo chimed in. <*One of them flickered during the jump, and the black hole spun out of place.*>

<*I've got it!*> Potter said. <*Stop trying to reset the thing, I*

can manually finesse it back into place.>

<*OK, hands off here,*> Bondo said.

Heather held her breath as the alarms on the bridge continued to blare. Ona and Garth shared a concerned look as the *Lance* continued to drift toward the planet.

<*Jump successful,*> Ferris's voice came to Heather a moment later. <*Escort moving into Delta formation.*>

<*Spread it out,*> Heather ordered. <*We're having black hole issues here. Don't want you to get eaten if we do.*>

<*Shit, seriously? It's loose?*>

<*OK,*> Potter announced. <*We're in the clear. It was one of the stasis field generators. It spiked a grav emitter during the jump, and then the one in the DMG chamber tried to compensate. I* ***cannot*** *believe they were planning on flying these things through gates without AIs.*>

<*Maybe they weren't,*> Heather suggested as the boards on the bridge began to flip back to normal status. <*Are we at risk of more problems when we activate our stasis shields?*>

<*I don't think so,*> Bondo replied. <*Just so long as we don't plan to fly through any black holes any time soon.*>

<*Noted,*> she replied to the engineer before addressing Ferris and the other destroyer commanders. <*Crisis averted, we're good to go. Assume Delta, let's see what the Niets are up to.*>

A series of acknowledgments came from the ten destroyer commanders as Heather strode to the holotank, scowling at the display as it began to populate with the position of the ships and stations in Chad's nearspace.

"OK…that's a bit more than we expected."

"Wow, is there some sort of party here that we didn't know about?" Ona asked. "I count over a hundred Niets…a lot of cruisers!"

Heather widened her stance and glared at the holotank's display as though it had personally insulted her. "Not like it's going to matter. Those Niets so much as fire a bullet at Chad, we hole them. Potter, let's do a broadcast."

<You got it. We're linked up to the relays and on the systemwide channel.>

Heather squared her shoulders and faced the forward optical pickup.

"Nietzschean scum. I can't tell you how pleased I am that so many of you have decided to hasten your own funerals. I'd worried that we'd get here and the party would be over, but it looks like you've not even started, and that is very, very good. Let me be clear. Every ship that fires on Chad, or any other target in the system, will be on the receiving end of a shot from our primary weapon. Trust me, one shot is all it'll take. You have ten minutes to get on an unpopulated outsystem vector." She took a step back and lowered her brow. *<OK, Potter, kill it.>*

The AI cut the transmission, and Heather turned to Garth and Ona.

"Well? Too strong?"

Garth twisted his lips. "Well there's the whole part where this thing's firing rate is pretty damn slow. A lot of them could get away before we could shoot them down."

Heather shrugged. "That's what Ferris's destroyers are for."

"Oh, we're being hailed," Ona said. "Should I put it on? Seems to be an Admiral Marsai."

"Do it, Chief. Let's see what the Niets have to say for themselves."

A woman appeared on the forward holodisplay a second later. She was tall and well-muscled, her jawline flexing as she stared at Heather as though her gaze alone could kill a mech.

"Umm...hello?" Heather said after the admiral stood silent for several seconds.

"Oh!" Admiral Marsai adopted an expression of mock surprise. "You're actually in charge there? I didn't know that the Genevians trusted mechs with ships."

"Well," Heather tilted her head and let a smirk settle on her lips. "Since most of our vessels are ones we stole from you, no one much cares if we dent them a bit."

"I recognized the craft," the admiral replied. "They were building that ridiculous monstrosity in Genevia last time I was there. I'm surprised it can even fly."

"Me too," Heather laughed. "But here we are, and it's time for you to surrender." While speaking to the admiral, Heather sent Ona a question. <*Which ship?*>

"I don't think that's going to happen," Marsai replied. "You're outnumbered eleven-to-one. Not even your special shields will hold up to that."

"Oh she's going to be in for a surprise," Garth whispered to Ona.

Heather didn't address the chief, keeping her eyes on the Nietzschean admiral. "Should be interesting to find out. You're down to seven minutes, by the way."

"Do you really think we'll just leave? Nietzscheans don't flee before Genevians. Especially mechs."

"Is it bad form if we shoot at her before the time elapses?" Heather asked Ona.

"Ummm…probably, ma'am. But...well, they are just Niets. I don't know that anyone will really blame you."

"Stars, I suppose you think you're funny," Marsai ground out the words between clenched teeth. "You have five minutes to surrender, or we open fire."

"Surrender?" Heather laughed. "Tell me about a time when mechs have surrendered."

For a moment, the admiral's haughty expression faltered, showing a worry layered behind it. But then her sneer came back, and she took a step toward the optical pickups. "Four minutes, thirty seconds."

The display blanked out, and Heather turned to Ona. "Bring up our stasis shields, I—"

<*Ma'am?*> Bondo called up from engineering. <*Remember how I said not to get us involved in a shootout just yet?*>

Heather pursed her lips. <*Umm..yeah?*>

<*Well…don't get us involved in a shootout. We can project a stasis field in front of the ship, but that's it, so….*>

Heather sighed as she watched the Nietszchean ships

begin to move away from Chad and array themselves before the small group of Marauder vessels.

"Oh shit." Heather muttered. "Maybe I shouldn't have pissed off the Niets."

<*Might have been prudent,*> Potter commented.

"Plotting course adjustments to keep the enemy in front of us, ma'am," Chief Garth announced.

"I have target lock on Admiral Marsai's ship," Chief Ona said.

A cruel grin split Heather's lips. "Fire."

The *Lance*'s main weapon powered up, fueled by a pebble of uranium dropping into the black hole in the DMG chamber. Exotic energy flared to life as the matter was ripped apart, and the black hole spun up, releasing twin jets of energy that were harnessed by the chamber and fired through the ship, at Admiral Marsai's cruiser.

It was as though the ship didn't even have shields. The blast hit the vessel on the port side of the bow, tearing a hole diagonally through the entire craft and exiting at the starboard engine.

Secondary explosions rippled through the hull, and a minute later, there was nothing left but a spreading cloud of debris and plasma.

"That'll—" Heather's triumphant utterance cut off as the enemy ships began to spread out, jinking as they approached the Marauder fleet.

<*They're moving to flank us,*> Potter advised.

"You don't say," Heather muttered. "Ona, time to fire the main gun?"

"Thirty-two seconds, ma'am," the woman replied. "The secondary DMG firing chambers are primed, though."

"Target the destroyers at the leading edge of their formation," Heather ordered, then addressed the ten destroyers. "I want a screen of grapeshot on our flanks. Keep those Niets from coming around."

<*Berra Station is coming around the planet,*> Potter said, shifting the secondary holotank to show a wider view of the battlespace.

Heather gritted her teeth and nodded, reviewing the details on Berra. Before the war, it had been a station that processed and disseminated the agricultural yield from the planet below; reports had indicated that it was now the primary defense platform for Chad, and scan supported that.

The station was heavily shielded, and had fourteen rails that could lob one-ton slugs at several hundred kilometers per second.

"Shit," the colonel muttered, knowing that in ten minutes, she'd be flanked by a station of all things.

Moreover, she couldn't fire on it, as Berra was packed full of civilians. Any shot that could penetrate its shields would rack up a death toll in the tens of thousands.

<*Ferris,*> she called out to the captain of the *Undaunted*. <*Is Third Platoon locked and loaded?*>

<*They're mechs, ma'am. They were born locked and loaded.*>

Heather rolled her eyes, but couldn't help a smile.

<*Take the* Fearsome *as an escort to Berra, and get Fuller's 'toon on deck. I want those rails offline yesterday.*>

<*Tall order, how's about five minutes ago?*>

<*I'll take it, Captain.*>

<*You're wish is my command, Boss Lady.*>

Ferris signed off before Heather could remind him to use rank. She considered sending the man a reprimand, but decided not to, knowing it wouldn't do any good.

The holotanks showed the two ships peeling off and boosting toward the station, which was half a light second closer to the planet.

A dozen Nietzschean ships shifted vector to intercept the Marauder destroyers, but the ships' stasis shields weathered the barrage inflicted on their port sides, while the vessels fired missiles from their starboard tubes that arced around to slam into the enemy ships.

Both groups were moving slowly across a fifty-thousand-kilometer stretch of space, and it was like watching an ancient naval fleet firing cannons broadside at the enemy.

"Ona," Heather nodded to the chief. "Lighten their load a bit."

The *Marauders' Lance*'s DMG weapons were still recharging, but the ship still possessed hundreds of beam weapons and two dozen railguns. Ona selected the optimal firing pattern, with a few suggestions from Potter, and twenty seconds later, ten rail-fired slugs streaked through the black, a shot aimed at each of the Nietzschean ships harrying the *Undaunted* and *Fearsome.*

The enemy ships were moving slowly, and only three managed to evade the slugs. The other seven saw partial shield failures, which were immediately exploited by the *Lance*'s beam weapons.

Thirty seconds later, four of the ships lost engines and ceased firing, while three were holed, but began to move away on their own power. The final three, two heavy cruisers and a corvette, continued firing on the pair of Marauder destroyers.

Then the *Fearsome* broke formation and boosted toward one of the heavy cruisers, opening fire with its forward beams and rails.

The Nietzschean ships pummeled the *Fearsome,* and Heather began to grow concerned as her readings estimated that the ship's CriEn module would be at max draw.

She was about to order Ona to direct more fire to aid the *Fearsome,* when one of the heavy cruisers lost shields and went up in a nuclear fireball.

The corvette broke off, and the remaining heavy cruiser began to boost away in its wake, moving back toward the main fleet formation.

"Thanks stars for small miracles," Heather said as the *Fearsome* moved back into its escort position on the *Undaunted*'s flank, and both ships continued to accelerate toward Berra Station.

She turned back to the primary holotank, which showed the remaining eight destroyers now arrayed in convex formation in front of the *Lance,* engaging with the leading Nietzschean ships, a formation of thirty-two destroyers and light cruisers.

"They're too close to target with the DMG," Ona said. "Their entire fleet is staying away from the business end of our ship now."

"Expected," Heather replied with a nod, scowling at a trio of heavy cruisers on the edge of the enemy fleet that had extended their AP nozzles and were boosting toward the *Lance.*

<I think they're planning a close pass,> Potter said.

"Or worse," Heather muttered.

The enemy had to have realized that the super-dreadnought was protecting its flanks, and was moving to exploit the fact that the *Lance* could not turn to face this new threat.

*<Bondo...**now** can you give me the good news?>*

<Good news? We managed to avoid a blowout in the ventricle power grid that almost took the forward stasis shields offline. How's that for good news?>

"Shit," Heather muttered aloud, knowing that, without the forward stasis shield, the enemy would tear the *Lance* to shreds in minutes. *<So I assume that means we can't get full coverage anytime soon?>*

<Dammit, Heather, no! Stripes and I just learned some fun things about firing a DMG through a hole in stasis shielding that will probably interest the ISF a lot, but is bad news for us.>

<OK,> Heather replied. *<I'm sending Crunch's squad to engineering.>*

<How's that meathead going to help?> Bondo snorted.

<He's going to make sure that the boarders we're about to take aren't going to kill you while you hold this tub together.>

<Oh….>

Heather killed the connection to engineering and turned to Captain Karen, who had been standing at the back of the bridge, hunched over a holotable with First Sergeant Aaron at her side.

"You two ready?" she asked.

The pair looked up, and Karen nodded. "You want Crunch at engineering, right?"

"He's closest, and we can trust his squad to keep the wrench jockeys safe."

"Agreed," Tex said with a nod. "We're going to have Lieutenants Fuller and Wilson cover these bays." He highlighted a series of large bays that the Marauders had picked out as the ship's most vulnerable breach points.

"And Lieutenant Chris will take the rest of First forward to protect the bridge," Karin added. "The Niets are gonna have to send a shit-ton more squishies than they can fit on three cruisers if they think they can dislodge a company of mechs."

"We'll take out as many as we can," Heather replied. "What about the starcrusher?"

"Yig's team has it on the hull already," Karen replied with a grin. "That thing is ridiculous, they're firing at starships and scoring hits."

"Tell them to hold their fire for the Nietzschean assault craft," Heather instructed. "From what we know about those heavy cruisers, they can sling a few battalions' worth of troops at us."

"Bring it on," Tex growled.

"I appreciate your eagerness to get in the fight, Sergeant," Heather grunted. "But the paint's still wet on our hull. Let's not mess up my new girl too much."

Karen laughed and shook her head. "Messin' up's what mechs do, Colonel."

WORM GARDENING

STELLAR DATE: 06.08.8950 (Adjusted Years)
LOCATION: Royal Palace, Mount Genevia, Belgium
REGION: Genevia System, New Genevian Alliance

Rika ambled down one of the lower passages in the estate that she was forcing herself to think of as the Royal Palace. For all her outward acceptance of her fate as magnus and—if her Marauders had anything to do with it—queen, her personal feelings on the matter seemed to waver on an hourly basis.

Mostly, the whole thing felt like hubris.

What I want more than anything else right now is for our fleet to be forming up in front of the gates and jumping to Pruzia to cut the heart out of Nietzschea.

The governance of the Genevian people was nearly anathema to her, but at the same time, she knew what would happen if she wasn't at the helm: snakes like Oda and Arla would slither out of their holes and try to sink their teeth into whatever would get them back in power.

They're as much our enemy as the Niets…maybe more.

<*Definitely more,*> Niki commented. <*Poison is always to be feared more than the overt threat. It's much harder to defend against.*>

Rika nodded. <*And exhausting. And annoying. What does it say about me that I'm spoiling for a fight, Niki?*>

<*That you're a woman of action.*>

<Sort of, yeah. But I've spent way more time idle, flying between systems.>

<I guess because you were always training? Maybe you should join in with your Marauders in combat sims.>

A sigh slipped past Rika's lips as she turned into the lower kitchen. *<I wish. Just too many meetings.>*

<You're an L2, now. You could multitask. Or I could monitor the meetings while you get in the sim.>

<That feels disrespectful.>

<It probably is. Does that make it wrong?>

<Yes, I suspect it does.>

Rika pulled her thoughts back to the world around her and surveyed the kitchen. There was an executive lounge three levels above, but that was where the nuevo-elite of the Genevian System were congregating, talking politics and policy. Rika was full up on that, and just wanted a peaceful meal.

"So you just gonna stand there like a Niet staring down a K1R, or you gonna have some food?"

Rika turned toward the familiar voice and shook her head, smiling at the sight of Kelly and Silva sitting at a small table at the edge of the kitchen.

"Why am I not surprised to find you two down here?" she asked.

"Beats me," Silva replied before picking up a piece of chicken and taking a bite. "We're sure as hell not going to be in the hoity-toity lounge up top."

"Plus, I'm the head of the Queen's Guard," Kelly added. "So I have to be where you are."

Rika eyed the SMI's bone-covered plate. "So were you checking it out in advance of my arrival?"

"Exactly," Kelly replied. "I had to make sure the food is safe, too."

"And?"

Silva snorted. "Safe, yes. Abundant? That's another question."

Rika sat in a chair next to the other two mechs, turning it so her back was to the wall. The moment she got settled, a cook appeared, a look of concern on his face.

"Your Majesty, is there something the matter with the lounge?"

"No," Rika shook her head. "Not with the lounge or the food it serves, just need a break from the company."

"Of course," the cook ducked his head. "I'm honored to have you in my kitchen. How may I serve you?"

"Stars, man," Rika shook her head. "For starters, you can treat me like you would these two. I came down here to get away from all the bowing and scraping."

"Careful," Kelly warned. "He almost kicked us out."

Rika glanced at the cook, and he gave her a crooked smile. "I might have threatened it."

"So has this been your job for some time?" she asked him.

"Oh no, my…I'm sorry, what title should I use?"

She reached out and gently patted his arm. "To you, I'm Rika. I didn't get your name."

"Rika." He said it slowly as though he were trying it

out for the first time. "I'm Faze. Head chef in the palace."

"Did you work here before the war ended?" Rika asked.

"No, I was living in Gerra back then. The Niets relocated my entire station's population to Belgium here after the war, and I've been working my way up ever since. I have a restaurant in Jague, but when the Nietzschean emperor came, I was brought here to run the kitchens."

"Shit." Rika shook her head. "I hope you know you're not required to stay now if you don't want to."

"Rika!" Kelly hissed. "Don't do anything hasty till you try his wings. The rub he uses is worth killing for."

Faze held up his hands and shook his head. "Oh, no, I've been hired on properly now. Chancellor Tremon himself extended the invitation."

"He must have tried the chicken, too," Kelly said as she reached out and grabbed a piece off Silva's plate.

"That's good," Rika said. "I guess I'd be silly not to give your wings a shot."

"I'll send over a platter," Faze said. "Hopefully I can impress you with something a bit more complex later."

"I look forward to it," Rika replied. "Oh, and a beer…whatever you think will go well, but nothing too hoppy."

"Yes, Your—Rika."

The cook blushed and rushed off, while Kelly chuckled softly.

" 'Your Rika'. That should totally be your title."

"Careful." She fixed Kelly with a baleful glare. "As your queen, I can levy some pretty harsh punishments."

"Oh? Like what?"

"Make you be queen."

"Gahhhh." Kelly slapped a hand over her heart and threw her head back. "You've found my weakness. Responsibility."

Silva snorted. "We've known that for years."

Rika nodded vigorously, and a pout formed on Kelly's lips.

"You two are always ganging up on me."

Another chef set a platter of wings lined with dipping sauces in the center of the table, and then another placed a plate and a glass of beer before Rika.

"Thank you," she said before smirking at Kelly. "What can I say, you're an easy target."

"Just for that, I'm taking the best sauce." The corporal reached out and grabbed one of the cups, setting it on her plate and hunching over it protectively. "Just try me."

"OK, OK," Rika held up her hands, sharing a smile with Silva. "I'll be nice. I don't want to upset my guard."

<*Which you really need to formalize,*> Niki added.

"What? Are you saying that Kelly, Keli, and Shoshin need to sleep sometimes?"

"It's overrated," Kelly said around a mouthful of chicken. "Of course, Jenisa should be in the guard."

"I'd hate to break up her fireteam," Rika said. "But I also know she'd kick my ass if I didn't induct her."

"Induct?" Silva laughed. "All your fancy meetings are really starting to do a number on you."

"Stars," Rika muttered. "What's happened to me? I need to fucking get real. Fuckity shit damn fuck poop."

"Poop?" Kelly snorted. "Yup. You're doomed."

"I recommend against that," Silva added.

"Being doomed?" Rika asked.

"No, fucking poop."

Rika groaned. "What would I do without you two?"

"Easy," Kelly said, grabbing a handful of chicken. "You'd be dead."

"You're such a peach."

* * * * *

The three women sat together long into the night, eating and laughing and drinking. Eventually, Chef Faze insisted on them eating a real meal and prepared a four-course affair that had them stuffed to the chin by the time they were done.

The hour was ticking over into the next day when Rika finally rose from her chair and bid the other two goodnight.

"You sure?" Kelly asked. "There's another platter of wings coming."

"Stars, woman." Rika shook her head. "If I never see another wing again, I'll be a happy mech."

"Liar," Silva winked. "Get your beauty rest. Tomorrow's the last day before you get coronated."

Rika cocked an eyebrow. "Is that the right word? Shouldn't it be crowned?"

"The crowning is the event where you actually get the crown placed on your head. The coronation is the whole ceremony. Hence, when it is done, you're coronated."

Rika was tired and a bit past buzzed, so she decided not to argue with Silva.

<There's actually some debate about that word. It's pretty ancient though, you can just claim that someone once used it that way, and we'll be good.>

<I wasn't really going to stress about it one way or another,> Rika replied as she took a deep breath and walked out of the kitchen.

"Don't do anything I wouldn't do!" Kelly called after her, and Rika waved a hand at the mech before turning down the hall.

<I suppose I should try to sober up before turning in.>

Niki sighed. *<You have ISF nanotech. You can sober up in an instant.>*

<Yeah, but where's the fun in that? Besides, it's almost impossible to get a good buzz on, I'm going to enjoy it while it's here.>

The AI made a sound that Rika took to be acquiescence as she wandered to a lift, which she rode up to the upper levels. Few people were around, and while most were polite and deferential, none engaged her in conversation, which was fine by Rika.

She reached a balcony that faced east and stared off into the deep, starry night, watching the light of starship engines and stations as they moved across the sky. In the distance lay the stars of the Praesepe Cluster, further away than she'd ever seen them before.

"I wonder if they're still building that ring around Pyra," she whispered into the night, then remembered that the light she was seeing was hundreds of years old.

<I imagine they are,> Niki replied. *<From what I've seen, the ISF tends to finish what it starts.>*

"I've noticed that, too. We're too far away to make out Albany, aren't we?"

<It's there, next to that blue giant,> Niki highlighted the star. *<You can just barely see it.>*

"And to think, all this started there when Leslie pulled me out of that pod."

Another star was highlighted on Rika's vision. *<Caulter. Technically, everything started there—at least for Rika the mech.>*

"Why not go all the way back to Earth?"

<For what?>

"For where it all started."

Niki sent a soft laugh into Rika's mind. *<That's where it did for me, you know. Well, not Earth, but Sol. Not a lot of us survived those early days, though.>*

"I can't imagine what that must feel like," Rika said. "To know that you've outlived…well, *everyone*."

<Hey! Be nice. Besides, there are humans older than me in the Transcend. Finaeus, for example.>

"Sure, keep using him as your out. Still…I'm sorry."

<Sorry for what? I've had a great life, and now you and I

are looking at something even more amazing.>

"And terrifying," Rika added.

<*Yeah, that too.*>

"Really?" she straightened and cocked her head. "You're terrified, too?"

Niki snorted. <*Imagine you were around for pretty much forever, but your fate is to merge your mind with a child's.*>

"First off…*hey*. And second off…no, just hey!"

<*Sorry, I couldn't resist. Trust me, I love the fact that you're young and vibrant. It's given me a new lease on life. I was…getting really bored. Not only did encountering you connect me to Bob and Tangel, I got a sense that there really is a purpose for all this.*>

"Really?" Rika asked as she gazed up at the stars. "I wonder about that sometimes. What are we all here for? Humans and AIs are spreading across the stars, but for what reason?"

<*Probably none,*> Niki replied, her tone turning fatalistic despite her prior statement. <*I've never seen one, at least, and as you like to remind me, I've been around a bit.*>

"So if there's no purpose, what is the point?"

<*What's gotten you all fatalistic all of a sudden?*> the AI asked, sounding concerned.

"I'm just looking at everything laid out before me and wondering if it's going to be worth the struggle." Rika pursed her lips and turned, leaning back against the railing. "Seriously, though, you must have some sort of idea what our reason for being is."

<*What is the purpose of an ant?*> Niki asked.

"I don't know." Rika shrugged, wondering about how ants saw the world. "To keep the colony running, I suppose."

<But is that their deep, meaningful role in the universe?>

"Maybe they don't have one?" Rika asked.

<They support the whole. Both the whole colony and the whole of life in the galaxy.>

"And what about us? We're at the top of the pyramid, are we just supporting the whole?"

<Maybe our purpose is to spread ants across the galaxy. Or worms. If you think about what humans are doing, you're really just earthworm-spreading machines.>

Rika considered the AI's words and shook her head, laughing softly. "That's a crazy thought. All our wars and struggles just to spread worms."

<Worms outmass all other life combined in the entire galaxy. Think about it. In a billion years, just about everything humanity has made will be gone—except there will still be planets everywhere with worms living in them.>

An image of a massive ball of worms drifting through space came to Rika, and she closed her eyes, an amused smile on her lips as she shook her head. "That's…huh…that's actually rather probable, isn't it?"

<That's why I said it.>

"But seriously, what about an afterlife? Gods and heavens and all that? A lot of people believe in that stuff, you know."

<I know. And they could be right. Stars, with what we've seen of ascended beings, a lot of 'gods' need to up their game to

compete. But here's an interesting thought. Even if there is an afterlife, what is it granting you? Eternity? Eternity of what? Hopefully it has some sort of goal, because having a goal and a sense of purpose is what keeps us going—both humans and AIs. It's what we're wired for.>

Rika snorted. "So what you're saying is that we could all die and go to heaven and still find ourselves asking, 'what's the point'?"

<*That's one possibility. I guess what I'm saying is that, unless you have some deity come along and tell you exactly what to do, you're going to have to find your own way. Find your own reason for being here. Even if it's just to spread worms.*>

"Stars, I'm sure glad I had this chat with you. The wisdom of ages is to spread worms."

<*Glad I can help. Oh, and try to be nice to people around you. That makes worm-spreading easier.*>

"What if instead of being nice, I make worm food out of people?"

<*You know, that's the best part of being an AI. I don't have to worry about what will eventually eat me.*>

Rika groaned and pushed herself off the railing. "This conversation has really not yielded the results I was hoping for."

<*That's usually a sign that it's time for bed.*>

"Yeah," she found herself stifling a yawn. "Chase is probably waiting impatiently for me."

<*He's working on the décor in the ballroom.*>

"Dear stars…what is going on with my life? I need to

kill some Niets, and soon!"

<Don't worry, they're still in good supply.>

A NEW CHARIOT

STELLAR DATE: 06.08.8950 (Adjusted Years)
LOCATION: Hanging Gardens Station, Babylon
REGION: Genevia System, New Genevian Alliance

"So," Kora leant her elbows on the galley table and folded her hands under her chin. "You're telling me that this Rachella from the PLI on Chad essentially blackmailed you, making you fly here to warn us about the attack there?"

The man gave a laugh that was half nervous, half rueful self-reflection. "When you put it that way, it seems a bit suspicious…and maybe it is. At first, I thought she was aboard just to make sure we'd come here and sound the alarm, but then she wanted to come all the way into Hanging Garden just to refuel. Now that she's gone…I dunno. Definitely something else at play."

<He's being really accommodating for someone smuggling people into the system,> Gary commented.

<Well, he had her on vid when he sounded the alarm to help Chad. Not really 'smuggling'.>

<Or maybe it's the best form of smuggling. Right out in the open.>

Kora glanced at the ship's first mate, a hard-looking woman named Avi. "What do you think of Rachella?"

"Didn't like her," Avi shrugged. "Wasn't too keen on her goons, either, but in the end, we got off Chad and out of Burroughs without too many scratches."

"I don't know if I'd go that far," Rajiz groused. "We still had to repair the engine while in the dark layer. Not my favorite pastime."

"Says the one who didn't have to go out into the dark," Avi replied.

"I would have," Rajiz shot back. "You and Gero are just better at that than Betty and I."

"OK," Kora held up her hands. "Seriously, you two, can we focus?"

"Well, what else do you want to know?" Rajiz asked. "We delivered the message, the Marauders—presumably—saved the day, and our spy lady slunk off somewhere. Isn't that what they do?"

Gary laughed. "Yeah, in my experience, they do."

"What about Belfas and the *Jay Rig*?" Kora asked.

"The whosawhat?" Rajiz glanced at Avi, who shrugged. "We have no idea who that is."

Kora watched him intently as she responded. "It's a resistance ship and its captain. They were going to go to Burroughs, but instead, they came here. Docked right around the same time as you."

"It's a busy station," the captain of the *ViperTalon* shrugged. "I think three other ships were docking at the same time as us."

The detective pursed her lips and nodded. "OK, yeah, you're probably right about that. Still, more coincidence than I can ignore. I'm going to need you to stay put until we sort this out."

"Seriously?" Rajiz asked. "How long is that going to take?"

"A long as it has to." Kora glanced at Gary. "The lieutenant is going to stay aboard just in case you think of anything else."

<I have a few friends here I can get to help out,> Gary said.

<No one that might report you to the PLI, right?>

<They're family, don't worry.>

"Great, sure, why not," Rajiz shrugged. "The *ViperTalon* is really just a hotel in disguise."

"More like a hostel," Avi muttered. "A free one, full of vagabonds."

"It won't take long—I hope," Kora said. "I just need to pay a visit to another ship first, and then we'll see if we need to talk to you further. With any luck, this'll turn out to be nothing, and you can be on your way."

"Yeah, I've heard that before," Rajiz interlaced his fingers and stretched his arms out, cracking his digits' joints. "Well? What are you waiting for? Go on, do your investigating so we can get out of here."

* * * * *

"What do you mean the ship's empty?" Kora asked as she approached the crew standing near the *Jay Rig*'s airlock.

"Well, not *empty* empty," the crew's supervisor said with a sour grunt. "It has all the normal ship stuff in it…minus people."

"How did it dock, then?"

The woman shrugged. "Engines, I assume. We just service ships, we don't throw ropes around the hull and heave to."

"Any chance they just left before you got here?" Kora asked.

"Nope, we were waiting at the airlock when they latched on."

Kora shook her head. "OK, thanks. Mind if I go aboard and look around?"

"Knock yourself out. Nothing we can do till someone signs off on the resupply."

Walking onto the ship, Kora immediately noted that the *Jay Rig* was clean. Exceptionally clean. The registry said it was a sixty-two-year-old pinnace, but the interior didn't line up with that.

"Maybe they're just neat freaks," she muttered, knowing that it would be unlikely that she'd find any evidence of the mysterious Captain Belfas aboard.

After releasing a pair of small drones to survey the vessel, she walked down the single corridor to the cockpit, noting that three of the seats were still covered in plastic film.

"OK, a refit, then."

The ship's public network had only the most rudimentary log entries and information, but it did note that the current complement was only one crew member. Whether that was true or not was another question entirely. Kora flipped through the inventory, and it reported three EV suits in a nearby storage locker. Upon inspection, she saw that all three were still there.

Of course, whoever was aboard could have brought their own—or just altered the records.

She also considered that the ship had flown from Capeton to Hanging Garden on autopilot. NSAI were more than capable of doing that, and the onboard system could have faked a human during docking.

The ship had a second airlock on the port side, and she checked it for any evidence, though the only hint that it had even seen a human's presence was a scuff mark on the floor that could have been made by anything.

<*I need to speak to the HGS security head,*> she said to the NSAI that operated the station's administrative offices.

<*That would be Lieutenant Merl,*> the NSAI replied cordially. <*He is, however, busy at the moment. Can I help you with something?*>

Kora doubted it, but figured it couldn't hurt to ask. <*I need to see if anyone exited this pinnace on its port side.*>

<*I'm sorry, that's privil—*>

She interrupted the automation with her detective tokens and auth codes provided by Chancellor Tremon.

<*Checking logs. One moment.*>

<*Thanks,*> Kora said and waited for over a minute for the NSAI to come back. When it finally did, the response was not what she expected.

<*Hanging Gardens Station has no external monitoring at*

that berth. I'm sorry.>

<*None?*>

<*Not at this time, no.*>

Kora walked back through the pinnace to the docks where the service crew waited.

"Is there really no external monitoring in this section of the station?" she asked.

"Not for a bit, no," the woman replied. "A few days back, there was a fire in one of the relay nodes nearby, and the optics and a few other sensors for several berths around here went out. I think it'll be a few more days till it's fixed."

Kora blew out a frustrated breath. "OK, thanks."

* * * * *

<*Dara, why is the airlock closed?*> Becky asked as she palmed the control panel. <*Is it because of how sketchy this station is?*>

The lock cycled open and she set her bags down, tapping her foot while the pressure equalized.

<*And why is the ship not on station pressure? My ears are going to pop, and I hate that. We already matched once, why undo it?*>

No response came from her crew, and Becky's foot-tapping increased in tempo and intensity.

<*Dara! What are you doing? Taking a nap?*>

The inner door finally opened, and Becky stormed through, nearly running into a skinny, blonde woman who stood in the corridor with her arms crossed.

"Who the hell are you?" the *Slyfe*'s captain looked the woman up and down. "We didn't ask for a cleaning service, we have bots for that."

"I'm not here to clean the ship," the woman replied. "I'm here to review your credentials before you go to Belgium for the coronation ceremony."

Becky's eyes narrowed. "You are? I thought I was already approved. I mean, why would I need to have any credentials checked? Everyone knows who my wife is."

"Just policy right now," the woman said. "I'm Rachella, by the way."

"Great, well, what do you need? I have to depart in the next twenty minutes."

"Yes, of course, I was just about to go to your bridge to get what I came for."

Becky glanced back at the bags in the airlock and considered grabbing them, but decided to leave it for a bot. She attempted to connect to the ship's NSAI to tell it to take care of her purchases, but it didn't respond.

"That's odd," she muttered.

The woman sighed. "OK, I suppose that's about as long as I could pull off that little charade."

"What are you talk—"

Becky's utterance cut off as the skinny woman pulled a pulse pistol from inside her jacket. "C'mon. Let's get to your bridge. We have places to be."

She tried to access the station's network, but her Link

wouldn't connect to anything other than the shipnet, and nothing there was granting her any access. "What about Dara? Did you hurt her?"

Rachella snorted. "Hurt her? Why would we hurt our new crewmate?"

The statement didn't make any sense to Becky, but at a gesture from the other woman, she slouched through the passages until she got to the bridge.

When the door opened, she saw Dara sitting at her console with a dark bruise around her right eye. A man sat in the command chair, and he smiled at Becky as she entered.

"Ah, good, our guest has arrived."

"What are you talking about?" Becky demanded. "This is my ship! You need to leave now."

Rachella shook her head. "We're all going to leave together. We've got a coronation to get to, and you're our ticket in."

Becky's eyes widened as she realized what was happening. "You're kidnapping me!"

"Sure," Rachella replied with a shrug. "Call it that if you want. Belfas, we ready to go?"

"You bet. Jerry and Jim have secured things belowdecks." His lips parted, and a cruel smile settled on them. "Time to go kill us a mech."

* * * * *

<I can't find any sign of anyone having been on Belfas's

ship,> Kora reported to Gary from a nearby security office, where she'd been reviewing sensor data and optical feeds.

<*Starting to wonder if Rhon just sent us on a wild goose chase,*> Gary replied. <*Though we did get a bit of a windfall courtesy of a comm message.*>

<*Oh?*> Kora asked. <*What is it?*>

<*Well, that thing that our friends here on the* ViperTalon *stole was a case full of DT11 chips.*>

<*I'm just a beat cop, what the heck are those?*>

The lieutenant laughed. <*I keep forgetting you're just a kid. DT11s are what was used on the mechs for the compliance system that controlled them.*>

<*Oh…OK,*> Kora nodded to the security chief as she left his office and walked back out onto the commercial docks. <*But the mechs can't be controlled by that anymore, and the subsystem that was vulnerable to the KK100s is fixed, too…right?*>

<*That's my understanding as well. But….*>

<*But what?*> she asked.

<*Well, mechs are just humans, right?*> Gary explained. <*There's really nothing stopping people from using Discipline on regular folks. I'm not sure if the Niets were doing it on Chad, or if some crime lord wants to use it on their goons.*>

Kora shook her head and double-timed it down the concourse, headed to the *ViperTalon*'s berth. <*OK, let's secure this tech and get it back to Belgium for Rika's people to look over. I feel like we've gone above our paygrade now.*>

<*I'm with you there. Should I book a shuttle for our ride*

back after we pay those smugglers a visit?>

Kora considered that for a moment, and then a smile settled on her lips. <*You know…we probably shouldn't just let our friends on the* ViperTalon *wander off till we get all the way to the bottom of this.*>

Gary chuckled. <*And they* ***were*** *telling us how fast their ship is.*>

<*Let me just get a proper warrant, and we'll be on our way.*>

The soldier's chuckle turned into a laugh. <*You're the last person I would have pegged as a by-the-book cop.*>

<*Well, it's more that I want this to be air-tight so that Avi doesn't just shoot us. That woman has some icy eyes.*>

<*Yeah, noticed that too. She's glaring at me right now—you'd better hurry up.*>

TAKING THE FIGHT

STELLAR DATE: 06.08.8950 (Adjusted Years)
LOCATION: GMS *Marauders' Lance,* Chad
REGION: Burroughs System, New Genevian Alliance

"Hit!" Ona cried out as the *Lance*'s beams finally penetrated the lead cruiser's shields and burned away its ablative plating. Gouts of flame burst into space, and one of the ship's engines died, sending it into an uncontrolled spin.

<*It's bleeding dropships and pods,*> Potter announced.

Heather double-checked the heavy cruiser's trajectory, glad to see that it would pass a hundred kilometers over the *Lance*.

"Keep point defense on that thing," she warned. "They could still lob missiles at us."

"Aye!" Ona snapped off her response, focusing the *Lance*'s weaponry on the second Nietzschean cruiser.

Four of the destroyers were also engaging the enemy ships, firing with wild abandon at the cruisers, as well as at the stream of dropships headed toward the Marauder dreadnought.

<*We've taken out four dropships,*> Yig announced from the starcrusher that stood astride the *Lance*'s central hull. <*But three have already made it through the shields. I can't see them anymore from where we are, but I think they're about to hit the bays.*>

<*Thanks,*> Heather replied, glancing back at Karen and Tex. "Looks like the bays are about to get fun."

Tex snorted. "Niets are gonna wish they stayed in bed."

The display above the pair's holotable showed a series of tacnuke launches from inside the ship, and Heather couldn't help but laugh.

"Bitty, I take it?"

Captain Karen nodded. "Not like I could stop him if I wanted to. He uses up tacnukes like they're pulse rifle batteries."

Nuclear blooms lit up amongst the incoming dropships, shredding several, but the combat net lit up a second later with mechs engaging ships that had punched through into the bays.

"Second cruiser is holed!" Ona announced, and Heather turned back to the main holotank and saw that it was spraying pods and dropships into space so rapidly, it looked like the ship was breaking apart.

"Oh shit," she muttered. "It *is* breaking apart."

"Musta hit something good," Garth said. "Look, the third one is pulling away."

The news was only half good. The three heavy cruisers had launched so many dropships and pods that the tracking systems were having trouble following them all. Estimates were fluctuating, but there were at least two hundred dropships and over a thousand escape pods—all headed toward the *Marauders' Lance.*

<*Targeting systems are having trouble tracking,*> Potter

said. <*We can't hold beams long enough at this range to penetrate their hull.*>

Heather pursed her lips. The Niets had built the *Lance* to be the 'main gun' of a fleet, something heavily protected by dozens of destroyers and cruisers. She'd become so accustomed to having stasis shields that flying into the face of overwhelming odds with a ship that could barely maneuver on the best of days—and was sorely lacking in close-range defense beams—had seemed like a good plan.

Note to self: next time, jump in at least half a light minute from the enemy.

She shook her head, slowing her rapid breathing.

<*Lieutenant Carson,*> she called down to the chief engineer. <*If you don't get that shield up in…oh, about three minutes, you're gonna have to walk home.*>

<*Yeah, I see it…it's like Niet soup out there. We're almost there.*>

<*In time?*> she pressed.

<*Shut up, Colonel.*>

"They made it through!" Garth said a moment later, and Heather felt a wave of panic until she realized that he meant the *Undaunted* and the *Fearsome.*

Scan showed that the station would be able to fire past the *Lance*'s shields in eleven minutes.

"They'd better hurry up," she muttered. "We wouldn't want the Niets to kill us before the other Niets can kill us."

Karen snorted a laugh. "Best I can see, they're only

going to get a few thousand troops onto the *Lance.* That's not nearly enough."

"They only have to take out the forward stasis shield generator," Heather reminded the captain.

"CJ's got it covered," Tex added. "Going to take a lot more than a few thousand Niets to get past her squad."

The mech's words were punctuated by a shudder that ran through the deckplate, followed by a hollow thud echoing down the passageways outside the bridge.

"What—" the colonel began, only to be interrupted by Ona.

"Four dropships made it through. They hit just a hundred meters aft of us."

"Did they breach?" Karen asked, grabbing her GNR's barrel off her back and slotting it into place.

Ona nodded. "Bays A1 and A4."

<*There are hundreds of them,*> Potter added. <*They're making for the bridge.*>

* * * * *

<*OK, you bastards, you wanna live forever?*> Crunch cried out as the *Undaunted* tore through Berra Station's shields. The ship fired its lateral port-side engines and spun to face the station broadside, the starboard maneuvering burners kicking on a second later.

<*Good luck!*> Ferris called down from the bridge just as a-grav cut and Crunch's squad sailed out of the bay, their own thruster packs burning hard.

Sixteen mechs—down three from full strength, with Kelly's team still back on Belgium—hurled through space toward a docking bay protected by nothing more than a grav shield.

<*Whispers, knock on the door,*> Crunch ordered Corporal Al, and fireteam one/one opened up with beams and kinetics, their weapons cutting into the bulkhead to the left of the bay's entrance, tearing through plas and steel until they hit the grav emitters.

A section of the shield died a second before the mechs reached it, and they blasted through the decompressing air to land on the deck.

Maglocks activated, and mechs unleashed hell on the bay's automated defenses and a pair of station security who thought that their pulse rifles stood a chance against the heavy assault team.

Ten seconds after Crunch had given the orders to Whispers' team, the mechs had secured the bay, and the emergency shield had snapped into place.

Motion to his right caught the sergeant's attention, and he saw a group of ship technicians huddled under a cradle's arms.

"Take it easy," he called out. "You don't shoot us, we won't shoot you."

The three fireteams flowed across the bay, checking corners and blind spots, making it to the interior doors in a minute. Once there, they formed up, with one/one stacked on either side of the door, and one/three and one/four covering them from a dozen meters back.

Crunch dropped a hackIt on the door control, and a few seconds later, it slid open to reveal four station security guards in light armor, holding multifunction rifles.

One raised his gun to fire, while the other three flung their weapons to the ground.

"Drop it!" Crunch thundered, and a fourth rifle hit the deck a second later. <*OK, people,*> he said over the combat net. <*Everyone has their targets. Run and gun, we have ten minutes before they can fire on the* Lance.>

"Ree-kah!" the mechs bellowed.

Ten seconds later, the four security guards were standing alone in the corridor, the smashed ruins of their rifles laying on the deck in front of them.

Crunch joined in with Kerry's fireteam as they raced through the station, headed to the fire control center for three of the rails. They needed to go the one-kilometer distance across the station's superstructure, and then six decks down.

They encountered light resistance at first, but as they drew near the FCC, they rounded a corner to see temporary barriers and grav shields blocking the passage.

<*Back!*> Kerry ordered as a stream of weapons fire filled the corridor.

<*Shit.*> Crunch coughed a laugh as the deck and overhead began to melt in the intersection. <*Those bastards mean business.*>

Curtis glanced back over his shoulder, and the RR-4

banged a fist against the bulkhead. <*This shit's not reinforced at all….*>

<*Civvy station,*> Carla replied. <*You thinking we just go through?*>

The RR-4 nodded. <*Map shows a storage room here. Blow a hole in the wall, then set charges up right next to those asshats.*>

<*Do it,*> Crunch ordered. <*We'll keep them busy.*>

Carla and Curtis began to cut a hole through the bulkhead next to them, while Crunch, Kerry, and Ryan fired sporadically around the corner whenever the Niets' barrage let up.

The pair of mechs made it through and disappeared into the storage room, and Crunch lobbed a grenade around the corner to distract the enemy on the off chance they realized a pair of mechs was cutting through the bulkhead next to them.

<*Setting the shape charges,*> Carla announced. <*Fire in the hole in five, four, three, two….*>

Crunch braced himself, maglocking his feet to the deck a second before the blast shook the station.

<*The hell was that?*> Kerry demanded.

<*Umm…I think the blast took out one of their shield generators' SC batts,*> Carla explained. <*They're, uh…neutralized, though.*>

The sergeant led the team around the corner to see the remains of the Niets.

"Well, shit," he muttered aloud. "That's a lot of bits and pieces."

<Let's keep moving,> Kerry said. *<These rails are going to be in range in four minutes!>*

*****

"Shit!" Heather cursed as the ship's internal scan picked up another group of Niets moving down a parallel corridor. *<They're gonna flank us! Van, where the hell are you?!>*

<Coming! Just trying not to destroy the ship on our way through.>

<Screw that, we're getting hammered, do what you have to do!> Heather quickly realized that might be too much leeway for the mech. *<Just no tacnukes inside my ship.>*

<Of course not,> The Van replied with a laugh. *<I do have these lovely HE rounds, though…>*

A staccato beat thrummed through the deck, and she tried not to think of where the mech was shooting as she nodded to Karen and Tex. "I'll fall back to keep them from hitting you in the ass."

"Sure," Tex said as he tossed a pulse bomb down the corridor, adding a trio of shots that took out two Niets who'd been thrown from cover. "Three's overkill for this approach anyway."

Heather snorted and fell back, passing the entrance to the bridge, where Garth and Ona were still managing the external defenses—with Potter's assistance—and rounded a bend to move into the next intersection, ready to take out the flanking Niets.

The scan and optics in the corridor were dead, so she flung a passel of nano around the corner, only to get visual on a dozen Niets in heavy armor.

<*Shit, these assholes mean business,*> she sent out over the combat net.

After considering her options, Heather activated her stealth systems and crossed the corridor, watching the Niets reach the intersection and then turn left toward the bridge.

Once they'd all rounded the bend, she lobbed a grenade and opened fire with her beam rifle, relativistic electrons slicing through two Niets before the grenade went off, slamming another four into the bulkhead. At the front of their group, one of the enemy had the presence of mind to turn and fire.

"Fuck!" Heather swore, diving around the corner as a rocket flew from a launcher on his shoulder, streaking toward her position.

For a moment, she thought she'd cleared the blast, but then something grabbed her legs, and she slammed into the bulkhead. Scrambling away from the cross corridor, it took her a moment to realize that her legs were gone from the knee down.

A Niet appeared in the intersection, staring down at her legs, and Heather raised her gun arm, firing a stream of kinetic rounds at his groin, tearing through the joint and ripping his left leg off.

"How's it feel, asshole!" she shouted, the words dying when three more Niets rounded the corner, weapons leveled at her.

<*Down!*>

The Van's single word thundered through her mind, and she complied, laughing as shots streamed overhead, the barrage of HE rounds tearing through the Niets.

<*Should be six more,*> she advised The Van as he approached, reaching down to lift her up.

<*Get on my back, Colonel,*> he said, and she grasped a hard mount on his back and held on as he rounded the corner, his chainguns tearing through more of the enemies.

She rested her gun arm on the K1R's right shoulder and added her own fire, careful to keep her head from scraping the overhead as they smashed through the Niets and came back to the passageway that ran outside the bridge.

Tex and Karen had fallen back to the entrance to the ship's command center, a withering barrage of fire slamming into the ribbing around the doorway.

<*Stay back,*> The Van's voice boomed as he ripped an emergency bulkhead seal from its hinges and charged toward the Niets, using the door as a shield.

Heather screamed as she released a DPU round from her GNR before switching to the electron beam, the pair's shots tearing through the Niets, utterly decimating a dozen before the rest turned to fall back, only to get cut down in crossfire as Ainsley and Jenny flanked them, DPU rounds and beams finishing what The Van's HE shots started.

Thirty seconds later, the corridor was silent—barring the groan of overheated metal and weapons ticking as they cooled.

"Shit." Heather breathed the word. "That was fun…and destructive."

"You're welcome," The Van replied as he ducked through the entrance to the bridge and walked to the command chair.

Heather swung off his back and landed in the chair, her eyes widening as she saw that Berra Station was seconds away from being able to fire around the *Lance*'s stasis shields.

<Ferris, do you have status from Crunch?>

<Seven down, five to go. We're getting in position, going to see if we can block any shots.>

Normally that would be difficult to achieve, but with both Berra Station and the *Lance* moving less than a kilometer per second relative to one another, it was possible that the destroyers could block a couple of shots.

Weapons fire sounded in the corridor again, and The Van patted Heather's shoulder. "Stay put, Colonel. I got this."

He walked to the entrance, wrenched the door free, and stormed back into the passageway.

"Maybe we should get him a shield," Heather muttered, wondering how long it would take to repair the *Lance*.

<Station's fired!> Potter called out, and Heather sucked

in a breath, releasing it when she saw the rail shot impact the *Undaunted*'s shields, shoving the ship a hundred kilometers before the destroyer's engines managed to stabilize the craft.

"Any day now, Crunch," she muttered.

* * * * *

"Shit!" Crunch cursed as his fireteam rushed toward their target. Ferris had just relayed that both the destroyers had been pushed off course by rail shots from Berra. <*Thirty seconds, people!*> he shouted at his team as Kerry and Carla rushed toward a group of Niets, shrugging off withering fire and slamming into the enemy, pushing them into the bulkheads for Curtis and Crunch to target with beam fire.

Ten seconds later, the pair of mechs reached the room's entrance, and all Crunch heard was, "Touch that button, and I'll blow your head off!"

The other three mechs on the team cleared the hall before entering the FCC room to see Kerry and Carla standing atop a console, weapons trained on a group of unarmored Nietzscheans who were backing toward the far wall.

"Would you look at that," Crunch muttered. "Niets who actually know how to retreat. Too bad your commanders don't understand that…then you wouldn't be looking at spending the rest of the war in a Genevian POW camp."

"War?" one of the Niets bearing a captain's insignia said. "The war's over."

"No," Crunch shook his head. "It's just getting started."

* * * * *

<*Shields are up!*> Bondo called up to the bridge, relief clearly audible in his mental tone. <*We've got full coverage…and a lot of dead Niets down here.*>

<*Lotta dead Niets everywhere,*> Heather replied. <*Good work.*>

"Should I take us in, ma'am?" Garth asked.

A smile formed on Heather's lips. "Oh hell yeah. Let's show them what we can do."

The super dreadnought surged forward, engines driving it toward Chad, complete shield coverage giving them full maneuverability. The main gun fired twice more, taking out two Nietzschean cruisers in short succession.

"They're breaking off," Ona announced.

<*Ferris,*> Heather called to the captain of the *Undaunted*. <*Chase those bastards down.*>

<*Oh you got it, Colonel. What about Crunch's squad on the station?*>

<*We'll reinforce them, don't worry.*>

<*Not worried, just want to make sure he doesn't have to walk home.*>

Heather laughed and closed the connection before

switching to a channel with Berra Station.

<So, whoever is in charge there should probably surrender now,> she said. *<Power down shields and point defense, all that.>*

<Will your mechs stop rampaging across our decks?> a worried voice asked.

<Yeah, I think they're done taking your rails out, so any rampaging should be winding down. Who am I speaking to, by the way?>

<I'm assistant stationmaster Vince.>

<Assistant? What happened to the stationmaster?>

<She ran off when your mechs landed. Took a shuttle to the surface.>

<You Genevian?> Heather asked.

<I am. Born here on Chad.>

<So was I, Vince,> she replied. *<Let's make a point to meet up before all this is done, share a drink, talk about how to get things back to how they were. You make sure everything's shut down, and I'll tell Crunch that you're in command and you're our guy.>*

<Crunch?> Vince sounded concerned.

<Yeah, leader of the squad of rampagers we sent over there.>

The newly minted stationmaster made a choking sound. *<A single squad? That's all you sent? I thought the station was going to fall with the havoc they caused!>*

The *Lance*'s commander laughed. *<Yeah, we tend to make that kind of impression.>*

QUEEN

STELLAR DATE: 06.09.8950 (Adjusted Years)
LOCATION: Royal Palace, Mount Genevia, Belgium
REGION: Genevia System, New Genevian Alliance

"Do we really have to do this?" Rika asked no one in particular as she stood in an antechamber just off one of the Royal Palace's ballrooms, looking through the surveillance feeds at the mass of attendees.

"Have to?" Chase asked from where he stood at her side, a genuinely happy smile on his lips. "No, I suppose we don't *have* to. But we really should. Besides, I'd much rather call you queen than magnus. Then I can be your royal consort."

"Oh?" She turned toward him, looking over his gleaming white armor, which matched her own. "Consort? You don't want to go for king?"

"King?" Chase snorted. "Stars, that sounds like a lot of responsibility. I'll keep my sights a bit lower."

"You realize that we'd have to marry before you could be either, right?" Rika asked.

The man who had been at her side for the past two years barked a laugh. "Is that how you propose to a guy, Rika?"

"Propose?" she coughed out. "Well…I guess I could at some point. I'd always thought that a wedding was the sort of thing you do after the war, though."

"Or at least after your coronation," Tremon said as he

approached, resplendent in a deep crimson robe. "Let's get one ceremony out of the way before we plan the next one."

A snort came from behind Rika, and she turned to see Kelly covering her mouth.

"What?" the mech asked innocently.

"What's what, that's what," Rika retorted. "I know that laugh. You're already planning our wedding."

"Oh hell no, I was thinking about my own."

"*You*?" Rika asked. "To who?"

"Really?" Leslie shook her head as she approached the group. "Are you blind, Rika?"

"Ummm..." Rika looked from Kelly to Leslie, then at Chase and Tremon. "Have I totally missed something?"

The chancellor nodded. "You really have. Perish the thought that all our lives hinge on your powers of observation, My Queen."

Rika groaned. "Well? Is anyone going to tell me?"

"You're serious?" Kelly asked. "You haven't noticed?"

"That's it." Rika turned away from her old friend. "I'm not talking to you till after I'm coronated."

"Oh?" the SMI asked.

"Yeah, then I'll issue a decree forcing you to tell me."

"It won't work," Kelly countered.

Rika turned back to the door, on the other side of which waited a room full of people she didn't know—most of them, at least. "You all really aren't helping."

"Easy, hon," Chase placed a hand on her shoulder.

"This is going to be a cakewalk. Tremon's going to guide you through it all. Thirty minutes and it's done but for the drinking."

"I'm already ready for that part," she muttered.

"So are we all," the chancellor said. "You know, I was nicely retired before I met you, Rika."

"You were hiding. That's different."

The chancellor shrugged, a relaxed smile on his lips. "You say tomayto, I say tomahto."

Rika quirked an eyebrow at the man, glad to see him actually happy. In many regards, his time in Genevia had mirrored hers, insofar as unwanted added responsibility was concerned. But, for all her grousing, the Genevian people had been receptive to her, and positive in their reactions to having a mech as their magnus, and soon to be queen.

<*I can pull the fire alarm if you need me to,*> Niki said to Rika. <*There's still time to escape.*>

She sent a mental laugh her AI's way and shook her head. <*No, no need. I think I'm ready for this.*>

<*You sure? Because I really don't want to have to deal with you complaining about it for the next few years.*>

<*Oh for starssakes, Niki!*> Rika exclaimed. <*You!*>

<*Yes, me. I'm really something else, aren't I?*>

Rika didn't reply to the AI, and glanced at Tremon. "So, do you go out first? I have to admit that I wasn't paying much attention to the order of procession."

The chancellor shook his head. "Yeah, me first, then—actually, Niki can just tell you when you're on. Relax and go with the flow."

<Don't worry.> Niki said to the group. *<I'll drive Rika if she stalls out.>*

"Umm…because that's not disconcerting at all," Rika muttered.

At Niki's direction, she stepped out of sight before the doors opened, and Chancellor Tremon walked out. He was followed by Kelly and Silva, who looked magnificent in their white armor.

In a way, the ceremony felt a bit like a wedding to Rika. Instead of being married to Chase, though, she was being married to the Genevian people.

Even so, she'd walk down the aisle with him at her side.

The only thing that felt wrong was how few of her mechs were present. In fact, other than the members of her personal guard—the rest of whom were spread throughout the room—there were no other mechs on Belgium.

<Finding a time when everyone could be here just wasn't going to happen. You know that,> Chase said.

<What? Can you read my mind now, too?>

<I could tell by how you were looking around,> he replied, shooting her a curious look over her use of 'too'. Luckily Rika was saved from him bringing it up by Niki speaking up.

<You're up.>

Rika took Chase's arm, and the pair walked out into the ballroom.

The space was filled with Genevian leadership, from planetary governors to ministers to stationmasters—nearly everyone in the inner system who had been found to be loyal—and not a Nietzschean toadie was present.

The room was decorated in a style fit for a mech queen. The pillars that supported the roof were covered in sheaths reminiscent of Rika's own armor. They rose up to a darkened roof that was filled with stars and images of ships passing overhead, Marauder vessels doing battle against Nietzscheans in the faux night sky.

At the center of the room was a raised dais, where Tremon stood waiting for Rika. Kelly and Silva stood on either side, and Chase stopped at the edge as well, holding her hand for a moment before letting go.

<*This is it,*> he said. <*Good luck.*>

<*I'm gonna need it.*>

* * * * *

Kora strode onto the *ViperTalon*'s bridge and stood next to the captain's station, arms akimbo. "We in queue yet?"

"Yeah, using your name got us priority placement," Rajiz said, his tone carefully neutral.

Despite the fact that Kora and Gary had essentially commandeered his ship, the captain hadn't made a big issue out of it, and seemed resigned to the fact that he was facing another round of interrogations before—hopefully—being let go.

Avi on the other hand had been building up a solid grudge, her eyes shooting daggers at Kora every time they encountered one another. It had become so uncomfortable that Kora and Gary rarely left one another alone out of a growing concern for their safety.

"That's good," Kora replied, wondering how to broach the next subject with the captain and his first mate, certain it was going to rub Avi the wrong way.

"So, I'm curious if you checked the case with the Discipline chips in it when you first took it."

"What do you mean?" Avi snapped, her brows lowering. "Are you asking if I popped it open for a quick look-see when we were in the Nietzschean compound on Chad?"

"Yeah, or shortly after," Kora suggested. "I'm just curious if everything was in there, or if some things were missing."

"Not that I know—" Rajiz began, but Avi stood up and spoke over him.

"Kora, what in the effing stars makes you think we know so much about Nietzschean Discipline systems that we know what would and would not be in that case? We were hired to steal it, and we stole it. Job done."

"Don't you check to make sure that you grabbed the right thing?"

Avi shrugged. "I was told to get a case labeled DT11-142-X, so I got case with that label. It was sealed and Linked, so I didn't exactly want to crack it open with ten thousand Niets around to see if they'd notice."

"And later?" Kora pressed.

"I opened it," Rajiz said. "But just to check that it had stuff in it. I only knew what they were from my time in the service, I didn't inventory them."

"Why do you ask." Avi's lips settled into a sneer.

Kora fixed the woman with as unpleasant a look as she was receiving. "Why the core do you *think* I am? Because some are missing!"

"How many?" Rajiz asked.

"Three."

"So?" Avi folded her arms across her chest. "Aren't all those Discipline units old Genevian tech? I thought the Niets hated mechs and the Discipline system."

"They did," Rajiz nodded, his brows furrowed in thought. "They hated the modification of the pure human form, but they respected the warriors. Maybe they have some mechs in their military and these units are for them."

"Wait." Kora turned to face the captain directly. "I thought you just said the Niets hated Genevian mechs."

"Well, I didn't say that exactly, but I imagine a lot do. Either way, they used our own mechs against us in the war, I wouldn't be surprised if they did it again. There's still that planet in the Melburn System. People say it's been cleaned out, but I think a lot of mechs are still there."

"Shit," Kora muttered. "Rika will be interested in that."

"So what are you worried about specifically?" Rajiz asked. "The Marauder mechs have been altered. The chips won't work on them."

The detective drew in a deep breath and rolled her shoulders in a slow stretch. "That's true, but what if they use one on a human close to Rika?"

Avi blinked, her expression turning from haughty to grave. "You're thinking assassination."

Kora only nodded. "I need to relay this to Leslie."

CORONATED

STELLAR DATE: 06.09.8950 (Adjusted Years)
LOCATION: Royal Palace, Mount Genevia, Belgium
REGION: Genevia System, New Genevian Alliance

The ceremony had been blessedly short. It consisted of her reciting an oath of office that was similar to the one the presidents used to swear, and then Tremon placed a small circlet on her head.

As much as Rika wanted to consider it a foolish bit of pomp and ceremony, the feeds were alight with the pride her people had in having a warrior queen, someone who would bravely lead the charge against the Nietzscheans.

There was some grumbling, but Niki assured her that those not in favor of having a queen were a distinct minority.

After shaking more hands than she ever had in her life—most prepared to use their left, though a few still surprised by the gun-arm on her right—she'd retreated to a balcony to gather her thoughts.

"Queen Rika," a voice said from behind, and Rika turned to see a slender, dark-haired woman walk onto the balcony, left hand extended to clasp hers.

Her HUD gave the woman's name, and Rika extended her hand. "Becky, captain of the *Slyfe*." They shook. "How nice to see you here. Thank you for getting us the news from Gerra so quickly."

Becky's eyes grew cloudy. "I'm just sorry it wasn't better news. I can't believe what the Niets did there! I knew they were savages, but attacking innocent civilians like that…."

Rika withdrew her hand. "Well, we saw worse in the war—though not by much. The Niets hate to lose."

"Yeah…I've noticed. Even after you beat them here, they tried to steal that ship."

<Something's off,> Niki said privately. *<Her speech patterns seem different than what's on file from when she sent the message about the attack on Gerra.>*

<Could the differences be accounted for by stress when she first arrived?>

<Maybe. I don't have a baseline for her. Either way, something seems off.>

Rika gave a mental snort. *<Thanks for all the compelling detail.>*

<Happy to help.>

"Well, the *Marauders' Lance* is quite the ship. I can see why they'd want it back."

"It's big, sure, but it's really not that good in a fight, is it? Just a large target that's hard to move around the battlespace. That's why I like my *Slyfe,* it's quick and nimble."

"The Niets like to make big ships," Rika shrugged. "Just like their Harriets and the *Fury Lance*. Then, later on, they realize they're not that practical, and focus on their smaller cruisers and destroyers."

Becky nodded as though she had a solid understanding of fleet strategy and tactics—which Rika very much doubted the woman did. She seemed to just fly around, living off money given to her by her wife.

She wondered what it would be like to have no worries, no stress, not a care in the world other than where you'd dock next.

<*Boring, I bet,*> Niki said. <*It sounds like a life without purpose, which sounds like death.*>

<*Surely it couldn't be that bad to just go a little while without purpose,*> Rika suggested as Becky began talking about interesting ships she'd seen at various stations in the past few years.

<*Sure, if you're taking a break. But this woman isn't taking a break, her whole life is a vacation. There's nothing to take a vacation from, nothing to go back to when it's over—which is why it's never over for her.*>

Rika tried to imagine what that would be like, but couldn't begin to fathom it. Still, the idea seemed enticing, even if it were just something to try for a while.

<*See, you'd just be* ***trying*** *it, knowing that there are still other things you'd go back to if you didn't enjoy an eternal vacation. My money is on Becky here having nothing to go back to. This is as much meaning as life will ever have for her—provided she doesn't make a change.*>

<*OK, OK, I get it. Point made and taken.*>

<*Good, now shoo her off, she's going to bore me to sleep with her commentary on which were the prettiest hulls she's seen.*>

<*You're an AI,*> Rika chuckled. <*You don't sleep.*>

<*Exactly.*>

"...the hull was this amazing iridescent blue, it was so beautiful. Too bad warships can't be pretty like that."

Rika suppressed a laugh. "Well, it's hard to be stealthy when your entire ship is glowing."

"Maybe they'd think you were so sure you'd win any conflict that no one would even take a shot...like those brightly colored frogs."

<*Wow...that's rather insightful,*> Rika commented to Niki.

<*Stars! She's infected you!*>

Rika laughed. <*Stop being so melodramatic.*>

<*No, seriously, she got some sort of nano-agent on you. I didn't pick it up at first because it registered as no-threat, but then she added more and it activated.*>

<*Can you neutralize it?*> Rika asked as she took a careful step back from Becky, not wanting the other woman to realize that the ruse was up.

<*Yeah, but only because I'm me and we have ISF tech. If you were just a normal person...shit, you'd be dead.*>

<*Leslie,*> Rika called out, only to encounter a dampening field that blocked her Link connection.

"Please," Becky whispered, her carefully crafted look of benign interest cracking. "They're making me do this. I'm so sorry."

"Who?" Rika hissed, anger causing her cheeks to flush.

"The PLI...Rachella. She said you took her sister and

she wants her back."

Rika glanced around the balcony, scanning the area beyond the doors to see if anyone else was nearby. *Stars, Kelly, where are you?*

"How many are there?"

"Please, they put something in my head, it hurts so much when I don't do what they want."

<*No…*> Rika whispered to Niki. <*Do you think?*>

<*Touch her, I need to get a heavy dose of nano on her, see what's up.*>

Without a moment's hesitation, Rika took a step forward and reached around Becky, placing her hand on the back of the woman's neck.

As she was delivering a passel of nano, the captain of the *Slyfe* jammed the heel of her hand under Rika's chin. There were tears in her eyes, and she mouthed, 'Sorry'.

Then Rika's entire world turned into pain.

* * * * *

<*Silva, have you seen Rika?*> Kelly asked. <*I was checking on a suspicious-looking woman, and when I turned around, she was gone.*>

<*Everyone's suspicious here. How did you manage to single one out?*> the colonel asked. <*And why not just reach out to her?*>

<*Funny.*> Kelly suppressed a groan. <*And I didn't reach out because I don't want to have to admit to our new queen that I lost her on her first state event.*>

Silva sent a laugh. <*OK, I can see that. She's out on the east balcony, talking to the captain of the* Slyfe.>

<*That's Becky, right? She's the one that gave us the heads-up on Gerra.*>

<*One and the same,*> Silva replied. <*She…oh shit.*>

<*What?*> Kelly asked, but had her answer before the message had even been sent.

Rika and Niki's signals had dropped off the network.

<*Dampener,*> Silva said unnecessarily. <*We're under attack!*>

A second later, every member of the queen's guard was on alert, with Silva, Kelly, and Keli moving toward Rika's last known position.

<*I just got intel from Kora,*> Leslie joined in on the Guard's combat net. <*Some of these people might be chipped. Could be anyone.*>

<***Discipline** chipped?*> Kelly couldn't keep the note of incredulous dismay from her tone. <*How the hell did that happen.*>

<*Looks like Arla's people, making another play.*> Leslie provided details on a woman named Rachella and a man named Belfas. <*I don't have these two as having made it into the palace, but that doesn't mean they're not here. Assume that at least five people have been chipped as well.*>

Kelly sent an affirmative as she and Silva closed on the exit to the balcony where Rika had last been seen. She was three strides away when something slammed into her and knocked her to the side.

She rolled to her feet and squared off against a

massive man who didn't hesitate to fling himself at her once more. There wasn't room to bring her GNR to bear, so she grabbed her pulse pistol, jamming it between them, and squeezed the trigger a half-dozen times.

The man shuddered and groaned, but didn't release his hold. Out of the corner of her eye, she saw that Silva was also grappling with an opponent, and another—a tall woman with a menacing glower on her brow—was closing in.

The man was punching her in the face with one hand while the other was clamped around her neck. Neither tactic was doing more than annoy her, and she thrust her arm into the air and swung her elbows down on the man's forehead. There was a sickening crunch and he staggered back before falling to the ground.

"Gross," Keli commented as she raced past, Kelly right on her heels.

"Rika!" Both mechs called out as they saw their queen slumped over the railing, another woman at her feet.

"I'm OK," Rika said in a weak voice. "Bitch fired an EM burst right into my face."

<*Thank stars for ISF flowmetal skin,*> Niki commented, her tone filled with relief. <*I would have lost some memories from that, otherwise.*>

<*Found the dampener,*> Silva said a second later.

"Shit, Rika!" Leslie cried out as she swept onto the balcony, her jet black form barely visible in the day's fading light. "Who—"

"Becky," Rika said, pushing the figure at her feet

over. "Niki shut her down and disabled her D-chip. She's not a threat anymore."

"Kelly killed baddies, and mine is going to need a cruiser-sized dose of pain meds when he wakes up," Silva said as she walked onto the balcony.

"Mine's going to need a new head," Keli said with a laugh as she glanced back out into the ballroom where the regular guard—mostly consisting of rebel forces from Gary's platoon at the Refuge—moved the guests back.

"Palace is locked down," Leslie said. "If Rachella and Belfas are here, we'll find them."

"Oh we'll find them, all right," Rika said as she straightened. "They can share a cell with Arla. Stars, it's like these people *want* the Niets back in here. Who do they think is going to fight against them if the mechs are gone?"

"Rika!" Tremon burst onto the balcony with his personal guards, Yakob and Gloria a step behind. "Core, you're alright...what—?"

"More of Arla's people," Rika said. "Party's over, we need to examine the rest of the guests for Discipline chips, and get our survivors checked over and locked down."

"Oh crap," Leslie muttered. "The *Overwatch* just picked up dozens of ships in low orbit making for our position."

"Military?" Rika asked.

"No," Leslie shook her head. "Civvies."

IT'S A TRAP

STELLAR DATE: 06.09.8950 (Adjusted Years)
LOCATION: GMS *Asora*, near Orden Station
REGION: Genevia System, New Genevian Alliance

"Glad you decided to slum it with us again, Captain?" Chief Ashley asked as Vargo settled into his chair on the *Asora*'s bridge.

"Why wouldn't I be?" he asked, a brow raised quizzically.

She shrugged. "I dunno, what with you really being an admiral and all, I thought you'd want to be back with the brass."

Vargo snorted. "It's inevitable, but I want to stave it off as long as I can."

"Inevitable that you'll be back with the brass?"

"Yeah." He let out a long-suffering sigh. "I always reset, try to get back to the bottom where things actually get done, but sooner or later, I end up in charge of stuff. I was an admiral in the war, then I got out and ended up a governor, of all things. That was waaaay too much responsibility, so I got out and signed onto the Marauders as a shuttle pilot. Next thing you know, I'm running a destroyer and now a whole fleet division."

"Don't forget that little bit of time where you were magnus of all Genevia." Ashley gave a saucy wink.

"Worst ten minutes of my life," Vargo muttered. "Can

you imagine what would have happened if Rika had died just then?"

"Died?" The chief barked a laugh. "You were all in the Royal Palace…or estate, whatever it is. What could have happened to Rika?"

"Who knows…choked on a pretzel, had a chandelier fall on her head, anything."

"There were pretzels?"

"No, but there should have been. Would have made that whole dog and pony show a thousand times better."

Ashley laughed. "Stars, when they were assigning ships, I got the best one. I—oh shit, we've got company."

Vargo sat up and nodded as the forward holo filled with Nietzschean ships. "Rika called it. The Niets are sore losers."

"Must be ships from at least six systems out there," Ashley said. "Over four hundred."

"A lot of destroyers and patrol boats," Vargo commented.

The ships were over an AU away, and as soon as they jumped, they began to spread out, making for a number of outsystem stations and moons.

Vargo had expected that. The Niets knew—or they'd better, by this point—that going toe-to-toe with the Marauders would only end in defeat. However, the enemy still had numbers on their side, and the Genevia System was filled with targets they could strike. Vargo's goal was to bog the enemy down and ensure that they didn't get into the inner system.

His fleet consisted of twenty-three vessels, four of which were cruisers, while the rest were destroyers. Each one was a Marauder stasis ship, though further insystem, at the outer edge of the Outer Asteroid Belt lay another fleet consisting of Nietzschean ships that had been constructed at the shipyards in Genevia and crewed by former GAF personnel.

On the far side of the system, another Marauder fleet waited; Vargo wondered if they were getting a visit from the Niets as well.

He sent out orders to the ships in his fleet, most of which were already in position, protecting the targets he expected the Niets to go after.

Rather than waiting for the enemy to come to them, he ordered his ships to charge the enemy, closing the gap and hammering the Niets, keeping the approaching craft from turning and braking.

<Sir, we have an issue.>

The call came in from the *New Paula,* a cruiser protecting a large station named Orden. Following in the wake of Scarborough, Orden was a major trade center, and also contained several refineries that processed specialized ores for the Capeton shipyards.

<What is it, Bernie?> Vargo asked the ship's captain.

<There are riots on the station. Not sure who instigated it, but there's a group of anti-queeners making trouble. They've taken the station defenses offline and are broadcasting surrender to the Niets.>

"Oh for fuck's sakes," Vargo muttered. *<OK, you stay*

on close defense, and land a squad of mechs to get those weapons back online. We'll swing around and give your approaching Niets a little greeting.>

<*Thanks, Admiral.*>

"Captain," Vargo groaned softly before reaching out to Captain Buggsie. <*Hey, Bugs, looks like we're all that stands between Orden Station and certain doom. See those Niets heading toward it?*>

<*Yeah, looks like fifty ships. Why can't Bernie handle it? He on the head or something?*>

<*Riots onstation, he's their defense for now.*>

Buggsie sent a laugh over the connection. <*Sounds right, he's good for taking a broadside.*>

Vargo had no idea what that meant, but decided not to press for details. <*I want you to sweep around to their rear, target the cruisers. We'll do the same, but hit them from the side. Just keep the pressure on and don't let them brake. They're moving at point-zero-one lightspeed—that'll give them only a minute or so to engage with the station.*>

<*Unless they lob missiles,*> Buggsie countered.

<*Well, let's just hope the mechs get the station defenses back online.*>

* * * * *

If Piper had been the type to sing, he would have belted out a joyous tune as he sailed high over Belgium in command of a ship, a vessel of his own, fast, powerful, and carrying hundreds of attack drones.

Staying in geosync over Mount Genevia, his ship—the aptly named *Overwatch*—kept close watch on the Royal Palace and surrounding terrain. The mountain sat at the head of a long valley. It was a lone peak flanked by two craggy ridgelines, both of which rose higher than Genevia, protecting it from inclement weather.

The mountain for which the alliance was named didn't rise above the tree line, and the dense forests that lined its slopes were of some concern to Piper, as it was difficult to see what lay beneath them.

Though the mountain was covered in sensors, many had been destroyed by the recent fighting, and a careful enemy could work their way up to the peak without being spotted.

Leslie had both drones and some of the newly minted Genevian regulars patrolling the slopes, but the AI didn't trust either. Both could be fooled. So he watched like a hawk, waiting for a sign that the Niets were going to take advantage of the opportunity to take out Rika and much of the New Genevian leadership.

Not on my watch, Piper thought as he ran an active scan sweep around his nearspace.

Every ship that came within a light second of Belgium was subjected to the AI's prying gaze. He wasn't about to let anything slip past his detection web.

Privacy be damned this one night.

Several ships had registered complaints with the local STC, and they had passed them on to Piper. He scanned those ships a second time, sending some of his drones to each, escorting them away from Belgium for their trouble.

It was heavy-handed, and he knew it, but if someone wanted to take the mechs and New Genevia down a notch, this would be the night to do it.

He'd followed the coronation ceremony with a feeling of pride swelling in his core—or his analogy to what he imagined humans felt as pride. It was a sense of rightness, that after all Rika had endured and sacrificed, she would get the recognition she deserved.

More importantly, this was the night she would be granted the full authority in the eyes of her own people to continue taking the fight to the Niets. Not that she required their formal approval, but Piper knew from experience that it was always nice to have the support.

He was watching the ship bearing Kora and Gary begin its descent to the spaceport at the base of Mount Genevia, when an alert reached him that there had been an attempt on Rika's life.

There weren't many details, so he clung to the word 'attempt' as he reached out to Niki.

<What happened?>

<Arla's people—I guess they call themselves the PLI—just tried to take Rika out,> Niki replied, her tone more angry than belying any injury. *<They failed, and other than a headache and inflamed synapses, she's OK.>*

<What about you?> he asked.

<Me? I'm fine. Rika's noggin is well shielded. Thanks for asking.>

Piper chuckled at her choice of words. <*There aren't many of us AIs in the fleet—or Genevia, for that matter. We have to watch out for each other.*>

<*I'm too old for you.*> Niki sent him an image of a wrinkled crone wagging a finger. <*Don't be getting any ideas.*>

<*OK, Grandma, I—and there's the follow-up.*>

He passed Niki his scan feed, which showed forty civilian ships, mostly freighters with a few private vessels and one hospital cruiser mixed in, shift out of low orbits over Belgium and make for Mount Genevia.

<*Looks like it's not over yet,*> she said.

<*Good,*> Piper replied. <*Permission to engage?*>

<*Why do you think you're floating up there like a giant piece of bait? Give 'em hell.*>

The once-multinodal AI gave a gleeful laugh in response, surprised at how excited he was to begin his first major battle at the helm of his own ship.

Other than a pair of destroyers running on skeleton crews, which was the norm for much of the Marauder fleet, Piper's Harriet Class carrier was the only military ship over Belgium.

Despite Niki's words, his near-lone presence was more out of necessity than a desire to bait any enemies into attacking the planet or the ceremony below. They were weeks away from sorting out who was still loyal to the Niets in most of the system's police forces, which had grounded all but a few patrol craft piloted by resistance members who had earned Marauder trust during the uprising.

Piper reached out to those ships and directed them to keep other vessels clear of the battlespace, and engage any enemy craft around the perimeter, but to stay at a five-thousand-kilometer altitude. To the pair of destroyers, he sent orders to drop out of higher orbit and move in to flank the ragtag fleet that was descending on Belgium.

His other orders were for himself, delivered to the first three hundred drones in his ship's bays. Bank after bank of five-meter attack drones loaded up on the ladders and dropped from the carrier like a swarm of bees streaking out over the night side of Belgium. Their engines burned brightly, sparks of illumination twinkling across the dull glow from the rebel fleet moving toward the surface.

He didn't bother with any demands for surrender. Rika had already sent up her own missive—which had been ignored—so when his fighters were clear of any unaffiliated civilian traffic, he opened fire.

The PLI fleet's rearguard consisted of six large freighters. Two were insystem scows, each over ten kilometers long, and the other four were interstellar craft, only half the size of the others. All were loaded with tens of thousands of cargo pods, effectively creating ablative shielding that massed more than an entire dreadnought.

He swung a dozen drones around toward the engines of each ship, unleashing their beams at the craft, only to encounter stronger grav shields than he expected. None of his drones' beams penetrated, and he loaded up a hundred heavy drones into the ladders, while directing the *Overwatch*'s four heavy rails to fire on the two insystem freighters.

Before his rounds even leapt from the rail accelerators, hundreds of cargo containers on the freighters opened up, spewing drones into space. A quick calculation showed there to be over a hundred thousand of them. Most appeared to be smaller, only a few meters across, but they swarmed his initial wave of drones, wiping them out in seconds.

A second wave erupted from the crates, these ones blasting through the screen provided by their predecessors, and then seeming to break apart.

Well, that's just cheating, Piper thought with a sour laugh as he identified the mines that now lay between him and his prey.

Rather than wasting drones sweeping the mines, he directed his bots around the edges of the field, switching their targets to a pair of smaller freighters, while he turned the *Overwatch* and accelerated toward the minefield.

The drifting space-bombs lay only five thousand kilometers above the planet's surface. When the Harriet plowed into them, he was certain that to the inhabitants on the planet below the light from the explosions would be brighter than at high noon.

The carrier's stasis shields flared, and the CriEns

spiked their energy draw, but the ship behind the protective barrier barely registered a shudder on its a-grav-dampening fields.

Even after seeing us destroy the Niets, they have no idea how to deal with ships like ours.

Piper unleashed a third wave of drones to escort his heavy hitters, which had remained behind the *Overwatch*'s stasis shields while the ship plowed through the mines.

The enemy drones had moved to the perimeter of the battle space to engage the first wave of drones, and the first rounds from the carrier's railguns had hit the bulk freighters.

The enemy ships' shields had only barely managed to deflect the massive kinetic strikes. Then the heavy drones lobbed their first wave of missiles, and the shields collapsed, leaving the freighters' engines open for the escort drones to lase.

Fifteen seconds later—five minutes after the battle had begun—the two scows were dead in the water, slowly drifting toward the planet below.

Piper tagged them for the tugs that had begun to form up in high orbit, and focused his attention on the next four freighters. They fell to the same tactic, and with that, the screen of ships protecting the rest of the advancing enemy fleet was gone.

The pair of destroyers had taken out seven other ships, leaving twenty-five still headed for the planet's surface. The hospital cruiser was at the center of the enemy formation, and Piper tagged it as his primary target, sending his heavy drones, along with an escort of attack craft.

A dozen of the enemy freighters fell back to engage, beam fire between the PLI fleet and the drones creating an almost solid sheet of energy above the planet.

The range of mountains amidst which Mount Genevia rested was coming into view around the curve of the planet, and Piper expected the lower vessels to begin braking in order to have more than a minute to pummel the mountain.

None of them did, however, and he adjusted his assessment of their tactics.

<Rika,> he reached out to his commander. *<I believe they plan to drop assault craft on your position. I'm targeting their largest ship in order to decrease the number of troops who make it to your position, but be prepared for a fight.>*

<Piper,> Rika sent the word back along with a laugh. *<We're already fighting down here! Aren't you on the command net?>*

<Umm…am I supposed to be?>

<Stars, Piper, you're a ship commander. Get on the command net.>

The AI took a moment to wonder why he assumed the humans wouldn't want him on their primary network, and laughed at his own uncertainty.

Too long in the dark, Piper, too many bad habits formed.

He joined in on the network, and his laugh turned to a shocked gasp as the full scope of the attack unfolded in his mind.

FLYING MECHS

STELLAR DATE: 06.09.8950 (Adjusted Years)
LOCATION: GMS *Asora,* near Orden Station
REGION: Genevia System, New Genevian Alliance

"You hardasses wanna live forever?" Lieutenant Crudge bellowed as he turned and ran toward the bay's open doors with N Company's squad one/one following after.

He leapt into space, not even bothering to look back at the *New Paula* to ensure that the twenty mechs were on his tail. He might as well double-check that the star was still burning while he was at it.

The mechs would be there. They would always be there. That was what he loved most about being in Rika's Marauders. Everyone fought. No one stopped.

That one simple rule was exemplified by Rika herself, and in Crudge's opinion, it was why they won. Plus, no one wanted to look bad in front of the CO.

He cleared his mind of the sentimental thoughts and shifted focus to the target ahead: Orden Station.

Not caring about spin-grav, Orden was a sprawling mass of interconnected platforms that spread for hundreds of kilometers in every direction. The thing struck Crudge as an inefficient waste, but no one had asked his opinion.

Granted, no one on the station had asked him to come

in either, barrels hot and blazing, but he was going to do that as well.

<*Sergeant Bruce,*> he glanced back at the squad sergeant. <*See that bay a klick to the right? Drop one/four over there. If I remember this place from prior shore leaves, there should be some maintenance routes that will get them to that point defense array over yonder.*>

<*You got it, Elltee,*> Bruce replied before passing on the orders.

<*Damn straight I got it,*> Crudge replied with a laugh. <*Send one/three into the bay just above our position. Go with them and try to get to the auxiliary C&C for the defensive systems. I'll take one and two across the skin to the defensive arrays on our left—see if we can patch into them directly.*>

<*Taking the easy job, are ya, Lieutenant?*> Bruce asked as the mechs began to adjust their trajectories, angling to their assigned destinations.

<*Shut yer piehole,*> Crudge barked good-naturedly. <*You're gonna be all safe and sound inside the station while we're crawling across the surface like ants.*>

The sergeant only gave a laugh in response, and ten seconds later, clawed feet met station hull.

<*OK, you lousy tinheads.*> Crudge addressed his two fireteams while highlighting a hundred-meter bulge on the station two kilometers away. <*That sucker's our target. Corporal James, you take one/one around to the right and see if you can get to the maintenance access point. Corporal Skip, you and one/two are with me. We're gonna go right for the fire-control relays and see if we can't just run the thing on*

manual if we have to.>

A round of 'Ree-kah's met his statement, and the two fireteams split up.

<*Why didn't we just drop right onto the defense array and save ourselves the hike?*> Skip asked as the mechs loped across the surface.

<*Oh, I don't know,*> Crudge shrugged. <*Maybe because that thing has point defense beams that can slice us to ribbons.*>

<*But the station defenses are offline.*>

<*No,*> the lieutenant corrected. <*They're not firing on the Niets. That's a very different story. They could just as easily fire on us as* ***not*** *fire on the Niets.*>

<*Oh…*> The corporal sounded embarrassed. <*I suppose that makes sense.*>

<*Situational awareness, boy. Not everything's going to be in a briefing.*>

<*We didn't even* ***have*** *a briefing,*> the corporal replied. <*Sergeant Bruce just told us to get our gear on and meet him in the bay.*>

Crudge snorted. <*Exactly.*>

His pronouncement was punctuated by a heat signature tagging his , and he dove behind a raised ridge on the hull.

<*Contacts!*>

The other four mechs spread out, combat net lighting up with six origin points for the inbound fire. Working like the well-oiled machine they were, the mechs of one/one selected targets and unleashed a salvo of depleted uranium rods at each.

<*Hull crawlers,*> Private Nona, an SMI-4, announced. <*Nasty little things.*>

Crudge nodded as he rose from cover, watching for any movement on the station's hull, knowing that more defensive crawlers could appear at any time.

<*Looks like the traitorous bastards inside have the defensive NSAIs under their control. Orden might have some bigger defense drones. Not sure what the Niets would have left them with.*>

<*We sure they're traitors?*> Corporal James asked. <*Just took out our own group of the things. Why do they make them look so spiny and gross, anyway?*>

<*Discourage pirates from doing shit like we're doing right now,*> Crudge replied. <*And I know they're traitors because there can't have been enough Niets left on this station to pull off a coup. That means there have to be sympathizers.*>

Despite the certainty he spoke with, Crudge knew it was possible that there actually were enough Niets on Orden to stage a coup—he just didn't want his mechs to hesitate if any Genevians drew on them.

The billion or so Niets now living in Genevian space was a problem that people higher up the pecking order than Crudge were going to have to deal with. If it were up to him, he'd send 'em all packing back to the fatherland, but given that Rika planned to cross the border before long, there was no reason in sending the enemy reinforcements.

Should just lock 'em all up, or stick 'em in cryo, then put 'em on some freighters and send 'em into the black.

Cryo freighters were a common form of prison ship. Most automated, and most set to spend centuries in the black before returning—if they ever did.

He took a moment to wonder how many popsicle prisoners were drifting in the dark, then laughed at the moniker he'd just made up.

The mechs had made it almost halfway to the defense node, when one of its secondary guns powered up and swiveled toward them.

<*Look out!*> Nona shouted.

<*It's not gonna—*> The words died in Crudge's mouth when he realized that the weapon actually *was* going to fire on them—and the station beneath their feet. <*Move!*>

A proton beam streaked out from the defensive turret, striking the hull where Skip had been a few seconds earlier, burning through surface equipment and ablative plating. Another shot streaked right over Crudge's head, causing his EM deflection systems to spike as stray particles hit his armor.

<*Faster! Evasive!*> he ordered, and the mechs all fired their boosters, propelling themselves across the station until they were within one hundred meters of the array, and outside the gun's firing cone.

Nona had taken a glancing blow from the gun. One of her shoulder-mounted cannons was gone, and the left side of her helmet was warped and blackened.

<*Your brain still working in there?*> Skip asked.

<*Don't worry about her, Corporal,*> Private Lais said.

<She doesn't keep her brain in her head.>

Crudge snorted, and assigned Lais and Nona to cover the team's six while he and the other two mechs worked their way around the hulking defensive array toward where the signal relays should be nestled.

<James, what's the word?>

<Mostly just happy that you guys were the ones that gun was shooting at, LT.>

<Funny. Have you made your target?>

<We're at the maintenance lock,> James replied. *<Thing has windows on both doors, so we can see some defenders setting up. Kurt's planting a charge that will take out both doors and ruin their day.>*

Crudge considered the wisdom of decompressing a few corridors on the station, and decided that he didn't care much.

<Have at it. We'll be at the relay node in five. If you can't take the array's NSAI, we'll patch in there and fire on manual.> The corporal sent a snort in response, and Lieutenant Crudge shot back, *<What was that for?>*

<Just pictured you trying to manually get a bead on an approaching starship with some sort of crude holo-joystick.>

<Shit, Corporal, why do you think I'm packing this tactical NSAI on my back?>

<Exercise? Blowing in five.>

Crudge felt the smallest tremor in the hull beneath his feet five seconds later.

Then, James reported, *<Once the dying Niets stop flying past us, we'll be going in.>*

Skip snorted, and Crudge chuckled as well, tapping into the other fireteam's feeds to watch enemies streaming past the mechs, several without helmets screaming silently as they shot into space.

Then the mechs moved into the twisted remains of the airlock, kinetics streaking out from their weapons toward the few armored enemies who had managed to maglock to the deck before being pulled into the void.

He kept an eye on their advance, but focused on his team's progress. They'd reached an alcove in the defensive array, where the relays that connected each of the massive guns to the targeting and scan systems inside the station resided.

<*There are going to be turrets in there,*> he warned.

<*Reeeeally, LT?*> Nona asked in mock-fear. <*What we gonna do about them?*>

<*Throw you into the opening to see what their rate of fire is,*> Crudge grunted.

<*Always the sacrificial lamb, never the priest,*> Nona muttered.

<*Good thing I remembered to pack my foam bombs.*>

The lieutenant grabbed one of the small orbs from a rack on his forearm and lobbed it into the alcove's opening. As soon as it passed into the entrance, it cracked open and bubbled into a four-meter sticky ball that attached to the hull.

Before it was fully expanded, kinetic rounds and beams tore through the object, shredding it and leaving only a bit of white schmutz stuck to the station.

<*Shit…glad you didn't forget those things,*> Nona muttered.

<*Did you track the trajectories?*> Crudge asked. <*Or just stare dumbfounded at the weapons fire?*>

Nona's response was to leap across the alcove's opening, firing her e-beam at three targets before sending a pair of DPU shots after.

<*Half down. You think someone else can take out the remainder?*>

Crudge nodded to Skip, who followed her example, a straight line of blue-white lightning flashing four times. After waiting a moment, the lieutenant tossed another foam ball into the opening, smiling as it expanded and no rounds of defensive fire struck it.

<*OK, move—*> the words died in his mind as a kinetic blast struck the foam and blasted it out into space. <*Well, looks like there's something else in there.*>

<*You sure, LT?*> Nona asked. <*Think it's bad?*>

<*Shut up, Private.*>

Crudge hadn't wanted to waste any of his nano, but decided it was the most expedient option at this point. He deployed a passel into a sticky blob and whipped it around the corner.

The nano released optical sensors, getting a better picture of the alcove than the rough blueprints showed. It was fifteen meters deep and five wide. Several smoking turrets lined the side, but there were five more that hadn't fired in the initial salvos, and remained ready to take out the mechs.

<Target them and go again?> Skip asked.

<No,> Crudge shook his head. *<There might be more. The nano landed close to an access port, I'm sending it in for a breach.>*

Nona made a sound like she was yawning, but Crudge ignored her, sending the nano on its way, letting the tactical NSAI he carried control it.

While the computer did its work, he checked in on the other teams.

<We're outside the control center,> Corporal James reported. *<But they've got the thing sealed up so tight that blowing our way through is gonna do some damage.>*

<OK, hold off on that for a few more mikes. We may have the relays by then.>

<You got it, LT.>

<Sergeant Bruce?> Crudge asked the squad leader. *<How are things on your end?>*

The RR-4 took a few moments to respond, and when he did, his mental tone carried a note of frustration. *<Fuckin' Niets and sympathizers are screwing around with guerilla bullshit, blending in. We're nearly at our target, though. We've taken to a 'get the hell out of the way, or get shot' style of advance.>*

<Just…> Crudge was going to advise the mech to be sure of their targets, but he knew that his people would never fire on civilians without provocation. *<Keep on keeping on, Sergeant.>*

<You got it, LT. I estimate five minutes and we'll be getting things in hand at the target.>

Crudge sent an affirmation and then saw that the nano he'd sent into the alcove had disabled the remaining defenses. He gestured for the fireteam to move in and secure it.

<*How you doing down there, Crudge?*> Vargo asked. <*I don't know if you've noticed, but those Niet ships that are coming didn't stop anywhere for lunch.*>

<*No?*> Crudge replied as he followed his fireteam in. <*Did you try offering them a BLT? I hear that usually does the trick with the Niets.*>

<*They only like them untoasted, and stars know I won't do that.*> Vargo laughed, and the lieutenant groaned.

<*Don't you give me that. Hot and cold mixed like that is gross. Untoasted is the way to go.*>

<*Has anyone told you that you're a barbarian?*> Vargo asked.

<*Frequently. OK, we've breached the array with the best angles on the incoming Niets. Pass me targeting data, and we'll give 'em hell.*>

* * * * *

Vargo breathed a sigh of relief at Crudge's news and turned to Ashley.

"Feed the lieutenant priority targets and vectors. We'll let him hammer them from the station while we run defense for any incoming rounds."

"And missiles?" Ashley asked.

The captain looked at the forward display and set his

jaw as he saw a wave of missiles heading toward Orden Station.

"Damn," he muttered. "Gotta be a thousand of them."

"Something like that," she replied as scan completed the tally at one-thousand-and-sixty-three.

Vargo contacted the captain of the other destroyer. <*Looks like we've got our work cut out for us. You're on the spinward side, we'll take antispin. Let's keep that station safe.*>

<*You've got it, Grand Poobah. Not a single Niet will get through.*>

<*That's the worst one yet. And I'm not worried about Niets, I'm worried about their missiles and beams.*>

The other captain snorted. <*Yeah, yeah, of course. That.*>

MOUNT GENEVIA REDUX

STELLAR DATE: 06.09.8950 (Adjusted Years)
LOCATION: GMS *Pinnacle,* Babylon
REGION: Genevia System, New Genevian Alliance

"I'm tired of fighting on this damn mountain," Chase muttered as he strode down the corridor that led to the Royal Palace's uppermost landing pad.

"Oh?" Rika asked, glancing to her right at the man—the mech—she'd grown deeply in love with over the past two years. "We've only fought on Genevia once. How can you be tired of it?"

He laughed, the good-natured tones calming her nerves. "Well, you've been busy with all your important queenly duties, so you haven't been running as many sims as we have."

"Wait. Aren't you the head of my guard? Can't you just mandate fewer sims?"

Chase snorted. "Right. And then I'd have Silva and Kelly up my ass about not taking the job seriously. Trust me, it's easier to just run a ridiculous number of sims."

Rika only laughed in response as she reviewed the data flowing in on the combat net. Mount Genevia and the Royal Palace were protected by three layers of security. The first consisted of police from several nearby cities under Commandant Perin. They were stationed on the roads and in the woods on the lower slopes.

Currently they were holding back the encroaching enemy, but the enemy was bringing in more hardware, and she imagined that Barne would soon pull the police back.

The second layer of defense was made up of members of the New Genevian Space Force. Their numbers were small, but consisted of veterans who had been vouched for by mechs and trusted members of the resistance. Rika had hoped to deploy them to ships, but with most of her mechs shipping out to defend the surrounding systems and Genevia itself, the planet of Belgium was largely left on its own.

Her own guard and a few members of the palace's security team made up the third layer of defense. Aside from Kelly, Keli, Chase, and Silva, Barne and Leslie were onsite, as well as Corporal Harlan's fireteam. Barne had taken the K1R's team to the lower levels. The docking bays at the foot of the mountain had been opened up, and were the palace's least secure entrance.

A K1R, two AM-4s and an SMI would plug that hole nicely.

<Do you think they'll try to bring a strike force to the upper landing pads?> Niki asked.

"I just can't imagine they think they can get past all our lower defenses in a reasonable timeframe. Those ships are coming down with only one thing in mind. They plan to drop troops, and their best bet will be to land them on the upper pads."

"Anti-air is going to take a lot of them out," Chase

said as they reached the door at the end of the hall. "Unless they think they can take out the mountain's power systems down below."

"Harlan will have something to say about that." Rika pushed the doors open and strode onto the landing pad where two skyscreams waited. "Not to mention the improved SC Batts we installed. Going to take a lot more than a little power outage to stay our weapons."

Chase gave the fighters a mistrustful look. "I can't say I'm excited to have you take to the skies when we're under attack from said skies."

"Don't worry," Rika kissed his cheek before pulling on her helmet. <*Kelly will keep me safe. The best place for me to be when they're attacking the palace is not in the palace.*>

"Not very queenly behavior." Chase's words were laced with a note of knowing resignation. "And what if they figure out that it's you in the skyscream?"

Rika thought about that for a moment before speaking on the command net.

<*Leslie, what callsign are you using for me?*>

<*Callsign? Oh, you mean our codeword for you?*>

<*Yeah, that.*>

The woman snorted a laugh over the Link. <*Are you sure you want to know?*>

<*Trust me, you don't,*> Niki interjected.

<*OK, well, Silva just became that. If the enemy manages to crack our comms, they'll think I'm still in the palace.*>

<*Hey, whoa, what?*> Silva asked. <*That's a mighty big target you just painted on my back.*>

<You saying you can't handle some rebel civvies?> Rika asked with a snort.

<No need to say such hurtful things, Rika! I thought I was like a mother to you.>

<You are. Now use that mothering instinct to be a good decoy.>

As she spoke, Rika gave Chase a final wave and bounded toward her skyscream, slotting her arms and legs into the mounting system, which pulled them off and pulled her into the heart of the craft.

Finaeus had offered to upgrade the skyscreams to allow the mechs the ability to merge with them without removing limbs, but Rika had declined. There was nothing like *feeling* like you were the attack craft itself, its wings your own arms, its beams your claws.

Kelly was first in the air, and Rika followed after, streaking out over the edge of the landing pad, skimming treetops as she angled upward, hurtling her body toward the heavens.

The pad had blocked the sound of the battle below, but once over the slopes, the echo of projectile and kinetic rounds rose up to meet her, their staccato rhythms punctuated by periodic explosions.

Rika's suspicions were confirmed, and a few moments later, Barne sent out the command for the police forces to move back to the secondary line, letting the military forces move to the fore.

<Barne,> Rika called down to the general, *<Why not just let Harlan's fireteam go out? There's no way some ragtag*

group of rebels will take them down.>

<That ragtag group of rebels has over ten thousand troops moving up the valley,> he replied. *<We're going to draw them in toward the bays and then drop the hammer.>*

<Ten thousand! How the hell did we miss that?>

<I'm not entirely sure, but Leslie is seeing red. Either someone didn't do their job, or loyalties are a problem for someone high up the chain—or both. Don't worry, My Queen, we'll take care of them. You just make sure we don't get hit from above.>

<Not on my watch,> Rika replied, coming to grips with the fact that this was more than just an assassination attempt—it was a full-on coup.

As much as she wanted to drop down and strafe the enemy's ground troops, she shifted her focus to the skies above, where five freighters had made it past Piper's defense. They had just appeared on the horizon, bright flares from their engines lighting up the night sky.

<Which ones do you want?> Rika asked as the skyscreams tore through a thin layer of clouds, now only a thousand kilometers from the braking ships.

<You take the one on the right, I'll take the four on the left,> the other mech said with a laugh.

<Funny girl. I'll give you the two on the left, and whoever finishes first can take the last one.>

<A competition! I love it!>

Kelly banked away, and Rika continued to boost toward the rightmost ship. It was sleek for a freighter, its grav systems creating a low-pressure pocket for the ship to slide through. Targeting an emitter near the ship's starboard engine, Rika fired a salvo of rail slugs, following them up with a stream of HE rounds.

The kinetics weakened the ship's shields, straining the systems that were already pushing the planet's atmosphere back, and the HE rounds hammered their way through, hitting the graviton emitter and knocking it offline.

A second later, atmosphere tore through the opening and tore at the ship, dragging it sideways and swinging the other side around toward Rika. She was only fifty kilometers away, but it seemed easy to lock onto the ship's starboard emitters and repeat the shots.

The second shield umbrella went offline, and she tagged the target for the ground batteries.

Rika was onto her second ship when one-ton slugs slammed into the first freighter's engines, turning the ship into a ball of fire falling toward the planet.

The second ship was a tougher nut to crack. She lobbed rail shots at ship's rear umbrellas, but they were too tough to wear down with a single pass. As her skyscream shrieked over the freighter, Niki highlighted a section of its shields.

<There!>

Rika spotted the weak patch on the top of the ship. No critical systems lay beneath it, and time was tight before the enemy vessels reached the optimal distance to disgorge their landing craft.

Without another thought, she fired her electron

beams at the weak spot, and dove after, punching her skyscream through and sliding between the ship and its shields. Her beams raked the ship's hull, and she dove under the craft and angled toward its engines.

Point defense beams lanced out at her attack craft, several scoring hits, but most unable to track a ship moving so close to the hull. Firing on an emitter next to the engines, Rika killed the rear shields and tore through, passing out into the planet's skies and tagging the ship for ground batteries.

<*We're too late!*> Niki flagged a swarm of objects pouring off the freighter moments before the ground batteries hit it.

Rika swore as she realized they were drones. Kelly's second target was also bleeding drones, even as the ground batteries fired on it, holing the ship from stern to bow.

The fifth ship had fallen back, and half the swarm of attack bots fell back to cover it, while the other half swept in toward Rika and Kelly.

<*I'm tracking over five hundred of them,*> Niki said. <*Sure would have been nice if they'd brought these into play when we were fighting the Niets.*>

<*Either they didn't expect us to win, or they were holding back to do this,*> Rika replied, her response eliciting a snort from Kelly as the queen dove her skyscream toward a pair of drones, shooting one and grabbing the other in her craft's talons.

<*Like they had the foresight for this,*> she said. <*You know*

they were just cowards and held back. Now that they realize that sitting on their asses for a decade earned them no reward, they're gonna take their piece of the pie by force.>

<*That last ship is going to have their remaining ground troops. Target it,*> Rika instructed Kelly, ignoring the leading swarm of drones and heading for the second.

The ships had slowed their approach to three hundred kilometers per hour. They were only two hundred and fifty klicks from Mount Genevia, and Rika knew that they were down to the final minutes.

<*Piper,*> she called up to the AI commanding the *Overwatch*. <*What can you give us?*>

<*Sorry, Rika. I'm mired in a few thousand drones, and my two destroyers are blocking orbital shots from their cruisers. I'm at least ten minutes from offering help.*>

The AI sounded genuinely sorry, and Rika wanted to tell him it would be OK, when another voice joined the command net.

<*Rika? Do you need a hand?*>

<*Kora?*>

<*That's me,*> the detective said. <*I'm in a ship with decent guns. We're breaching atmo near your pos—*>

<*Go for the last ship. Ignore the fighters,*> Rika interrupted.

Kora laughed. <*OK, we're on it!*>

A streak of light lit up the horizon as another ship tore through the atmosphere and then rotated, firing its engines directly at the final enemy freighter.

<*A churn and burn on just one ship?*> Rika wondered if

the freighter could pull it off, but stared in awe as she watched the *ViperTalon* manage the maneuver.

<*One hell of a stick jockey to pull that off in atmo,*> Niki commented.

The *Talon*'s engine wash swept across the drones escorting the final ship, knocking dozens of them out of the sky. The enemy freighter fired back, but its beams couldn't push through the flaming wash in atmosphere, and the ball of fire streaking toward it carried on unabated.

After a few more seconds, the *ViperTalon* cut its burn and turned, its own beams raking the final freighter, but the drones took the brunt of the attack.

Rika boosted toward them, her own beams and weapons lashing out, felling drones as she went, but the leading swarm followed after, and she spent as much time battling them as the group defending the ship.

She monitored Kelly during the desperate fight, making sure her teammate was alright, slicing through attackers that were on her tail more than once. As they fought, the drones seemed to slow down to a crawl, their movements languid and predictable.

Rika lobbed kinetics and fired beams at weak points she identified, and the robotic attackers dropped from the skies in droves. Even so, there were still hundreds more, and a screen of them lay between her and the freighter.

A quick review of scan showed her that the ship's shields were nearly down, so she tagged it for the ground defenses to hammer.

The aerial battle was now only one hundred kilometers from Mount Genevia, and the six rounds from the ground defenses took only seconds to reach them.

Each one was blocked by swarms of drones that moved between the shots and the surface-to-air slugs.

Missiles streaked out from silos in the mountain, trails of smoke following their twisting paths, but only two reached the freighter.

Explosions blossomed in the night, and scan updated to show that the ship's forward shields were down. Rika didn't hesitate to boost forward, twisting through the beam fire that tracked after her from the drones.

Like before, they were too slow, easy to predict. She evaded their shots with ease and focused on the freighter's forward sensor domes, blowing them away before dropping to its hull, sinking her talons into the ship's ablative plating to slow herself down.

Letting go three seconds later, she spun and fired her missiles into the cowling around the freighter's engines. The ship lost power, and Rika mapped its trajectory, glad to see that it would pass over mount Genevia and land in the next valley—which was thankfully uninhabited.

<Shit, Rika,> Kelly complained. *<You're taking all the fun.>*

<Fifth ship was whoever got there first,> she replied. *<Besides, you seem to be enjoying tearing drones to shreds.>*

<*It's not the same,*> the other mech complained.

<*If you two will clear the skies, we've loaded grapeshot to clean out the rest of the drones,*> Barne growled over the command net.

Rika was about to respond, when the final freighter began to disgorge drop pods. She was prepared for landing craft, but not for the hundreds of pods now spewing from its belly.

<*Drop pods inbound!*> Niki called out on the command net, and passed updated targeting information while Rika and Kelly boosted away from the enemy craft.

<*Firing,*> Barne announced, and a haze of pellets streamed out from Mount Genevia.

The pods spread out, the remaining drones moving to the fore, protecting the attackers from the grapeshot. It worked for the most part. More drones fell from the sky, but other than a few casualties, the pods remained unscathed.

<*Fuck,*> Kelly muttered. <*They're going to make it.*>

The *ViperTalon* was firing from the rear, taking care not to shoot at angles that would hit the mountain and its defenders, and the two mechs in their skyscreams were doing the same.

It wasn't enough. Seconds later, over two hundred drop pods hit the side of the mountain.

<*At least they spread out to avoid our fire,*> Niki said. <*They're all over the slopes.*>

Rika saw that the AI was right. The enemy drop pods covered almost ten square kilometers of the eastern slopes of Mount Genevia.

<*They're above our line,*> Barne reported. <*And Harlan's team is engaged with the enemy's main force on the road.*>

<*Chase, how are things with you?*> Rika asked.

<*Silva and Leslie are dealing with some strays that made it up the slopes,*> he reported. <*Keli and I are moving to the eastern gardens with some of the palace security. The VIPs are all still safe, though they're rather frightened. They were pushing to be airlifted out till they saw the number of drones you were fighting up there—nice work, by the way.*>

<*Thanks.*> Rika held back a laugh at the thought of the Genevian VIPs pushing to leave the palace, then running back to hiding when they realized it was the safest place to be.

<*That's a bit mean-spirited,*> Niki commented.

<*Sorry, I get all predatory and cruel when I fly these things,*> Rika replied.

<*I've noticed.*>

She picked an outcropping three quarters of the way up the mountain and tagged it for Kelly.

<*I'm out of rounds, and my batts are running low,*> Rika said. <*I'm touching down here.*>

<*I've got some more ammo to spend in my 'scream. I'll cover you from above.*>

<*Just be careful,*> Rika cautioned. <*You'll be low-*v*. Those bastards will have some surface-to-air with them.*>

Kelly snorted. <*Not my first time out, Mom.*>

<*Queen, not Mom. I have more authority.*>

The other mech laughed. <*No one has more authority*

than my mom.>

Rika banked around the top of the mountain and swept down the slopes, releasing her last few missiles in the direction of the enemy forces, and then settled down at the rear of the outcropping.

Once her limbs were reattached, Rika jumped to the ground. As she did, Kelly's skyscream streaked overtop, beams flashing out, striking targets in the forest and setting a few dead trees ablaze. Rika grabbed a portable shield generator from the back of the 'scream and sprinted to the edge of the outcropping.

Mount Genevia was normally covered in sensors. Unfortunately, the assault led by her mechs a few weeks ago had destroyed much of the network. Small drones still provided some scan coverage in the gaps, but Rika knew that a determined enemy could slip past them.

However, unless the rebels were to circle around to the west side of the mountain—where they'd encounter Harlan and the bulk of the regulars—they would pass on either side of the promontory. And Rika would be ready for them.

ON THE SLOPES

STELLAR DATE: 06.09.8950 (Adjusted Years)
LOCATION: GMS *Overwatch,* Belgium
REGION: Genevia System, New Genevian Alliance

Piper sectioned off a portion of his mind to watch Rika and Kelly in their desperate defense. He felt guilty that the five freighters had slipped past him, but the PLI had sent in another wave of ships, and it had taken the last of his drones to stop them.

He had a few dozen bots, but they were consumed with mopping up the remaining enemy drones, as well as chasing after a few dropships the freighters had disgorged at high altitude before being destroyed.

Six PLI ships in the second wave had boosted back to a higher orbit, trying to blend in with the civilian craft at parking altitudes, and he'd dispatched the two destroyers under his command to chase after them.

That left him contemplating how to help with the situation on Belgium. Thousands of PLI troops were closing in on Mount Genevia; Rika and a few mechs were all that stood between them and the Royal Palace.

If it were up to Piper, he would extract everyone from the palace, and then nuke it from orbit.

With the enemy's orbital offensive in tatters, they didn't possess the ability to stop starfire from falling on their heads. The only problem was that the fighting on the mountainside had become a morass. Defenders were spread through the forest in pockets, holding back the enemy via overlapping fields of fire, but they were too close to the PLI troops to use any weapons of mass destruction from above.

I need to get closer.

The battle had taken the *Overwatch* five thousand kilometers away from Mount Genevia, and several thousand klicks higher above the planet's surface. Piper set a new course, turning the ship, and fired its engines to slow the craft's orbit and bring it closer to the ground.

Unlike the smaller freighters that had penetrated Belgium's atmosphere, the Harriet Class ship's engines possessed the thrust to reach geo over Mount Genevia in minutes, even in atmosphere.

Of course, running the fusion burners that hot deep within a world's gravity well could ionize large sections of its atmosphere, creating storms and even sparking wildfires from the heat.

Take it easy, don't kill all the organics.

<So, you're coming to help, are you?> Barne's voice rasped in his ear. *<Unless you have some sort of prior engagement. I wouldn't want to keep you from something important.>*

<You're funny, Barne,> Piper's tone was emotionless. *<Pass me targets, and I'll drop slugs on them.>*

<Keep it tight, our people are everywhere.>

<General, I managed blackholes at the center of moons in a klemperer rosette for centuries. I think I can lob a few slugs

without hitting any friendlies.>

Barne didn't respond, but a series of coordinates with safe radiuses followed a few seconds later. Piper could fire on four of them from his current position, and let loose with a salvo of kinetic rounds.

Each rail-fired pellet was just a few kilograms wrapped in a sabot that protected the slug during atmospheric entry. The sabots burned off roughly one hundred klicks above the targets, and from there, the depleted uranium rods fell on the enemies.

<Nice shots,> Barne called up a few moments later. *<The other targets are no good anymore. Move closer and I'll get you new ones.>*

<You got it, General.>

<OK—> Barne stopped. *<Shit, Rika needs help on the eastern slope.>*

Piper rechecked his velocity and firing angle. *<I'm six minutes from a firing solution. I thought the bulk of the enemy was coming up the west?>*

<Drop pods. Get there as fast as you can, but pick off any targets you can hit while you're on your way.>

<Yes, sir,> the AI said and shifted the Harriet's descent, bringing it in a slow arc around the western edge of the continent, taking care not to create too many storms in the wake of his ship's passage.

Both Rika and Leslie were on that mountaintop. There was no way he'd let either come to harm.

No matter what.

*****

Rika spied another group of rebels moving through a copse of trees on her right, and let fire with a depleted uranium round, the rod striking the leader and turning him into a chunky spray before tearing through the woman behind him.

<*I'm starting to feel bad,*> she told Niki. <*Half these idiots are in light armor. Who sold them this bill of goods?*>

<*Light armor or no, they've all got good weapons. Our shield's almost out of charge.*>

As Niki made the comment, another series of rounds slapped against the grav barrier. The field—which had been deflecting rounds a few minutes ago—only slowed these, and they tapped against Rika's armor before falling to the ground.

<*Kelly, get down here so we can use your shield,*> Rika ordered.

<*You got it, Queenie. Just got a group of these mofos in my cross hairs. Might as well use up my last rounds.*>

<*Queenie?*>

Kelly laughed. <*Yeah, I needed a nickname. 'My Queen' is too—*>

The SMI's message cut off, and an instant later, Rika picked out a fireball just over a kilometer away. It arced down toward the side of the mountain, plowing through conifers, before a cloud of earth shot into the air.

The debris hadn't even begun a downward arc before Rika leapt off the outcropping. The forty-meter trees below raced up toward her, and she grabbed onto the trunk of one, bending it before letting go and splitting her feet apart into her customary three-clawed appendages and grabbing hold of another.

A second later, she was on the ground, tearing through the foliage.

Rounds pinged off her armored body, and Niki highlighted the origin of the shots. Rika fired without even looking; only the cessation of the attack indicated she'd met with success.

More rebels appeared in the woods, weapons barking in the night as they tried to hit the SMI-4 dodging and weaving through the trees. Some she fired at, some she ignored, some she ran right over, her armored body crushing bones and tearing apart her enemy.

Ahead she saw fires burning amidst the trees, and she angled toward the light, finally coming to a stop in a deep furrow plowed into the ground by Kelly's skyscream.

The ship's central bulge appeared intact, but one wing was sheared off, and the rear section where Kelly's limbs were stored was a crumpled ruin.

"Fuck, Kelly, you'd better be OK," Rika muttered as she slid down the loose scree and then jumped atop the ship.

"I will be if you don't knock me loose and roll us down the mountain," Kelly's sarcasm-laced voice came from within.

Rika snorted, GNR whipping to the side, and fired an

electron beam at a rebel who appeared at the edge of the trench.

"Sure, that's our biggest threat right now."

The top hatch opened halfway and then jammed, but Rika grabbed hold and prised it free, revealing Kelly's helmeted head.

"You wanna go for a ride?" she asked the mech.

"I take it the fact that I can't get a response from the rear compartment means it's gone?" she asked.

"No," Rika shook her head. "Just doing an impression of a crushed can. Don't worry. I can carry you."

Kelly nodded, and the ship released the clamps holding her in place. Rika reached down and extracted her longtime friend, swinging her around and settling the other mech onto her hardmounts.

"Maglocks working?" she asked.

"Yeah," Kelly replied. "I'm your little mech barnacle."

Rika groaned in mock horror as she took stock of the surrounding woods. Downslope, things appeared to be clear, but there was no visibility on the other side.

<EMP took out our drones,> Niki commented. *<Surprised you didn't notice sooner.>*

"You're so gracious," Rika sighed as she released a pair of microdrones, flinging them into the sky. "Let's see what we can see."

The small bots took a minute to clear the debris and fire, whereupon they showed a force of a hundred rebels closing in around the crash site. More were visible in the distance, and Rika realized that fully half the enemy on the eastern face of the mountain was within a few hundred meters.

<Barne, I have a juicy target for you.>

<Can it hold a few minutes? Piper's bringing the Overwatch *around so he can target the eastern slopes.>*

<Can it ***hold****? Are you asking me to ask these PLI dorks if they can stand still for a bit while we get ready to shoot them?>*

The general groaned. *<You know what I mean. But I'll take that as a no.>*

<Yeah,> Kelly added. *<Big no.>*

<How long's a few minutes?> Rika asked.

<Coordinates?> the general asked.

<On my head.>

<Somehow I knew you'd say that. We're going to need five. I assume you won't be there by then?>

Rika wondered about that. *<When I say 'fire', you fire.>*

<Rika—>

<That's an order.>

There was a brief pause. *<Understood.>*

She climbed out of the gash in the earth, feeling an unspoken question from Kelly.

<I'm not going to call it down right on us. Niki dropped nano on your skyscream as well, and she's working on bringing its shields back online.>

<Rika,> Kelly cautioned. *<A strike that takes out a thousand enemies isn't the sort of thing a 'scream's shields can deflect.>*

<Right, hence the part where I don't call it ***right*** *down on*

us.> She reached the top of the earthen slope and climbed onto a felled tree, calling out as she did, "Who's in charge here? Bring them forward."

<*'Bring them forward'?*> Kelly asked with a snicker.

<*Sounded right in my head.*>

The enemy soldiers had the sense to remain in cover as she stood atop the smoldering log, her GNR pointed at the ground between them.

"Why should we do that?" a voice asked from behind a nearby tree.

"Because I'm Rika, Queen of New Genevia."

She felt like a fool saying the words. For all intents and purposes, she'd proclaimed herself queen in a ceremony meant to impress the populace. Instead, she'd shown that she couldn't even protect her own house.

"Queen." The word was spoken with a snort of derision. "Some queen."

"Queen of dirt," another rebel soldier said.

A laugh slipped from Rika as she glanced down at her once-pristine white armor, now covered in scorch marks and grime. "We mechs have a lot of experience with dirt."

"Fitting," a new voice said. For a moment, Rika's vocal analytics tagged the speaker as a high probability match for Arla, but when she spoke again, the system suggested a sibling. "It is, after all, what you were made for. Getting dirty."

"Are you trying to tell me that someone else's intent in my creation has anything to do with my destiny?"

Rika asked. "By that logic, no one should ever go against the will of their parents."

"I'm not going to argue your purpose with you, mech. You were made to serve Genevia, not rule it. You've had plenty of chances to return to your proper place, but you never took it. Now you'll be forced to."

"Oh for starssakes," Rika muttered. "Why do you people always have to talk like this? Do you think that you're somehow going to convince me to see the error of my ways? I've *saved* Genevia. I've taken on our enemies and crushed them. I've stopped your attack, too, even though you were working with the Niets."

"What are you talking about," the woman asked, stepping into view.

"Rachella," Rika hissed, recognizing the woman. "How did I not realize it before?"

"I hacked the *ViperTalon*'s comm systems. They shifted my voice and appearance just enough. I didn't know then that you'd imprisoned my sister, but I still knew better than to trust a mech."

Rika wished the woman could see the smile on her face. "Oh, you can trust me. To put you right where I put her."

"Where?!" Rachella demanded. "What did you do with my sister?"

"Oh, she's tucked away somewhere," Rika replied with a shrug. "Nowhere you'll find anytime soon, though." She turned her attention inward, to Niki. <*How're we looking?*>

<Thirty more seconds. I need to build a new bridge to the emitter.>

<I say you just shoot her,> Kelly said. *<I think her voice is built entirely out of registers designed to make me want to tear my ears out.>*

Niki chuckled. *<Good thing you have no arms.>*

<Small mercies,> Kelly grunted.

"Don't mess around with me, *Queen* Rika." Rachella spoke the words with clear derision. "You're going to free all your Genevian prisoners and then abdicate. We'll let you leave in exile if you publicly swear never to return."

"And my ships, my mechs?"

"They can swear fealty to a new government."

"Oh?" Rika cocked her head. "A democratically elected one?"

"Eventually."

"So how's that any different than what I'm doing? I don't want to be queen forever. This is just to strike fear into the hearts of the Niets. But the middle of a war is no time to hold elections." Rika turned as she spoke, taking in the soldiers arrayed around her, many peering out from their cover as she spoke. "We've pushed the Niets back. At this rate, we will topple them entirely in a matter of years. Then I *will* retire. I'll step aside, and we'll set up a new government. But for now, Genevia needs a single ruler, and like it or not, I am that person."

"You're not a person," Rachella said as she took a step back. "You're a mech."

<Niki…>

<I see it. I'm ready.>

<Barne, we're passing you targets. Just don't hit the center, and we'll be fine.>

<Shit, Rika…that's a hell of a payload.>

<I know, I set it.>

<We're still fifty seconds from firing.> Barne sounded nervous. *<Scan shows you completely surrounded.>*

<I noticed that too.> Rika couldn't help but be terse with the general. She knew he was worried about her, but it was the only way to buy time.

"I wish you hadn't come down here to get me," Kelly whispered. "I would have been fine."

"Like hell you would've," Rika whispered back. "You're my sister. I'll never leave you behind."

With those words, a stillness came over the woods, the distant echo of weapons fire faded, and the skies cleared, stars and ship engines shining through. Rachella took another step back, the movement slow and languid, as though the woman were moving underwater. At the same time, the rebels eased out from behind their cover, weapons sighting on Rika, faces grim in the dim light.

<Niki….>

Weapons barked, projectiles and beams streaking toward Rika, only to stop centimeters from her, halted by the skyscream's shield.

<I can only hold it out this far for a few seconds. Get back!>

Rika didn't have to be told twice. She jumped back, sliding down the embankment to where the skyscream lay. She looked up again and saw new lights sparkling in the night sky, long streaks heralding imminent doom for the rebel forces on the mountain.

<*Fuck!*> the AI swore.

Rika didn't have to ask why she'd cursed. The grav shield had failed.

<*My bridge burned out,*> Niki said, her voice a desperate whisper. <*There must have been an extra load on the circuit!*>

Rika didn't bother asking if there was time to fix it. There wouldn't be. What she did think about were the stories Silva had told her, of how Tangel and Cary could manipulate energy fields, how Cary had formed her own grav shield to protect herself from Myrrdan.

How did they do it? she wondered, sharing her thought with Niki via the channel the AI used to listen to her mind.

They think small? I don't know….

Rika thought about atoms, about the particles that made up neutrons, protons, and electrons, about the spinning donuts of energy deeper down, the base energy that created mass. It all seemed more real than ever before, not just a concept, but a base reality she could touch.

The way gravitons sped off the collections of energy-mass suddenly made sense to her, and she released a swath of them, watching the dirt on the embankment jump.

"Shit," she whispered, looking up at the incoming

rods from heaven that would surely kill her as well as the rebels.

Beneath her feet lay the skyscream and a few uranium rods that Kelly hadn't fired.

"It's been nice knowing you," the other mech now whispered in her ear.

"Hush, you. I'm concentrating."

A moment later, she'd tapped into the uranium, a dense wealth of protons and neutrons filled with mass. She twisted it, causing anti-gravitons to spray out. She held those in a field, trapped in place by creating an opposing force, the effect forming a shield over the gouge in the mountainside.

A second later, the fire from above struck.

Mounds of dirt, rock, and trees flew into the air as the rebel force that had surrounded Rika ceased to exist. The ground shuddered and groaned for what seemed like hours, but Rika knew to only be a few seconds. Then the aftershocks diminished, and she heaved the field outward, flinging away the debris that had fallen on her shield.

She sagged for a moment as the energy that had flowed around her dissipated.

"OK…how did you fix the shield so fast?" Kelly asked.

<*I didn't fix it.*> Niki's voice was mixed with jubilation and awe. <*Rika did that on her own.*>

"That? What that? You made the shield, Rika?"

After sucking in a deep breath and letting it out

slowly, Rika nodded. “I did.”

“Stars, woman, you can do shit like that? I think you’ve been holding out on me!”

REUNION

STELLAR DATE: 06.10.8950 (Adjusted Years)
LOCATION: Mount Genevia, Belgium
REGION: Genevia System, New Genevian Alliance

Rika stood on the balcony where Becky had tried to kill her only ten hours prior, watching the shadows in the valley shrink as the sun rose behind the palace.

Tremon had just left, informing her that the last of the VIPs had departed from the palace, its halls now empty of their complaining voices.

"No," she whispered. "That's not fair, many of them were thankful."

<Most were, really. Just a few were…stressed by the events,> Niki said. *<Can't blame them. It's been some time since they've been in the thick of things.>*

"Well, with any luck, they can go back to their idyllic lifestyles," Rika muttered, trying not to resent the fact that she seemed to suffer more problems at the hands of her own people than the Niets.

"Lives of rest and relaxation for everyone but us?" Chase asked as he walked onto the balcony and leant against the railing next to Rika. "Not that I'm complaining. I like kicking ass. Sleep when we're dead, and all that."

Rika glanced at Chase to see a sardonic smirk on his lips.

"You're not as funny as you think you are when you're tired," she said.

"Me?" He placed a hand on his chest. "I'm always funny. It's a part of my charm."

"No." Rika shook her head. "You're funny, and compassionate, and smart, and lots of other stuff, but not all of them all the time."

"Well, I'm understanding. That one I know for sure."

Their eyes met and held, gazes unblinking for almost a minute.

"I suppose you are," Rika finally said. "Granted, I *am* your queen, so you don't have much choice."

He coughed softly. "Kelly told me what you did down there, how you made your own shield."

There it is, she thought. *He's going to think I'm a freak.*

Rika hadn't worried about what Chase would think of what she'd done—not that she wasn't concerned, she'd just been too busy. But now, in the still morning with no one around, there was no running from it. She'd done something only an ascending person could do: matter manipulation.

"I don't exactly know how I did it—" Rika stopped herself. She did know exactly how she'd done it, she just couldn't explain it. "Not exactly…ish."

"Well, I imagine I wouldn't understand even if you were less -ish about your exactly." Chase smiled, his eyes filled with understanding, though a question lingered.

"I can see what you're thinking," Rika said. "You're

worried I'm going to turn into a ball of light and float away."

"Will you be a ball? I've heard stories about how Tangel and Cary get all tentacle-y. Like a big, white octopus."

"Are you making fun of me?"

He chuckled. "A bit. Maybe just trying to add some levity…for my sake as much as yours."

Rika placed an arm around Chase's shoulders and pulled him close. "Don't worry. I'm not going anywhere, and no matter what comes, we'll figure it out together."

"So, what *is* coming?" he asked.

Rika's gaze retuned to the vista before her, and she drew in a slow breath, a resolute look settling on her features. "I'm glad you asked. I want to accelerate our plans."

FORMING UP

STELLAR DATE: 06.11.8950 (Adjusted Years)
LOCATION: GMS *Marauders' Lance,* Chad
REGION: Burroughs System, New Genevian Alliance

"Shit," Heather muttered. "I'm from here, and even I don't know why the Niets fought so hard over Chad."

"Probably because what was left of their raggedy-ass fleet had already hightailed it out of Burroughs." Crunch grinned as he spoke, leaning up against Ona's console, earning himself a narrow-eyed glare from the woman. He ignored her. "Either way, I like it when they put up a fight. Then I don't feel so bad for kicking their asses."

"Would that stop you?" Captain Karen asked from where she stood staring at the holotank.

"No, probably not. I just like to feel good when I'm killing Niets. Well…more good."

"Comm drone just jumped in," Chief Garth announced. "Tokens check out, it's from Rika."

"Put it up, Chief," Heather said, rising from her command chair.

The Genevian Queen appeared in the holotank.

"Colonel Heather."

Rika looked tired, but there was a light in her eyes, something new, something hungry. Heather liked it.

"The Niets hit our outer system like we expected. Vargo and the others held them off, and Travis has squared things away in Gerra. We had a small insurrection here, but that's squared away now—just a last gasp from Oda and Arla's people. But their little attempted coup has solidified something in my mind. We're not going to waste time in Genevia any longer. We're jumping to Pruzia. It's time to finish this fight."

Rika's words elicited a round of muted cheers on the bridge, and Heather shared a look with Karen, both women wondering what was to come next.

"To that end, I want you to jump to Pruzia ahead of the main force. I'm sending you a series of targets in their outer system. You're to destroy them. Utterly."

"Shit," Heather whispered, knowing that Rika meant for them to use the *Marauders' Lance*'s main weapon to completely obliterate whatever they were sent after.

"We're going to show the Niets that it's over. They can pull their bullshit tactics all they want, but whatever they wreak in Genevia, we'll bring on them tenfold in their own star systems." Rika paused, her expression softening. "No need to be brutal. Give them fair warning, but make it clear. Good luck, Colonel. Good luck to you all."

For a moment, Heather was silent, considering Rika's words. Then she turned to Ona. "You heard the queen, Chief. Deploy the gate. Pruzia won't fall on its own."

* * * * *

THE END

Rika's dalliance in the Genevia System has come to a close. Rather than wait on rebels, politics, and the Nietzscheans to pick away at what she's built, the Genevian Queen is going to finish the fight in the heart of Nietzschea.

Click here to get the next book in the Genevian Queen series, ***Rika Destroyer***

MECH TYPES & ARMAMENTS

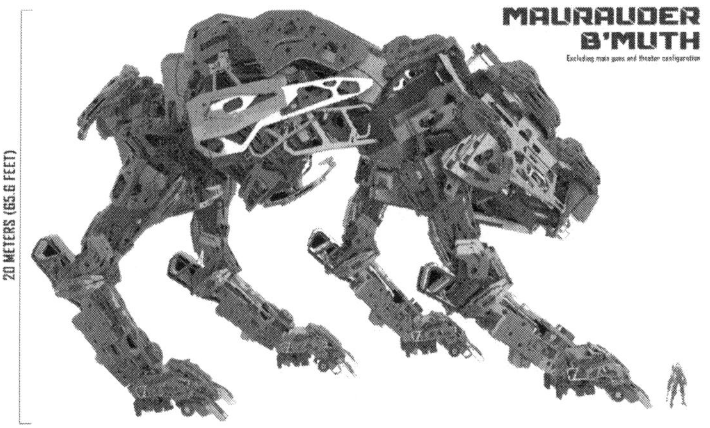

While these are the standard builds and configurations documented by the Genevian Armed Forces (GAF), many mechs reached the field in mismatched configuration, or were altered after deployment.

Sometimes these alterations were upgrades, sometimes downgrades, as repairs were often made with whatever spare components were available at the time.

The mechs in the Marauders generally align with the stated configurations, though many have altered themselves over the years.

NOTE: The K2R and all 4th generation models were made by Finaeus Tomlinson, in concert with Rika's Repair and Maintenance team, specifically Lieutenant Carson and Corporal Stripes.

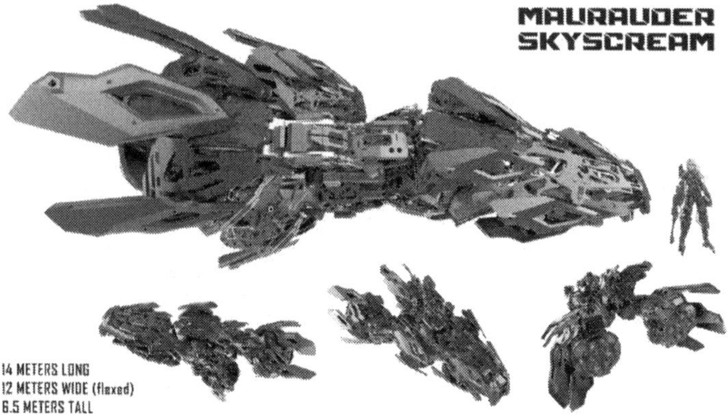
MAURAUDER
SKYSCREAM
14 METERS LONG
12 METERS WIDE (flexed)
6.5 METERS TALL

K1R (Kill Ranger - Generation 1)

This mech is more of a two-legged tank than a mech. The K1R sports a central 'pod' where the human is situated. None of the limbs utilize human material.

K1Rs often had mental issues due to feeling as though they had lost all sense of humanity. When the Nietzscheans won the war, they did not release any K1Rs from their internment camps. It is not known if they kept them, or killed them all.

Until the discovery of the mechs in the Politica, there was only a single K1R in the Marauders (who had been under General Mill's command at the end of the war). That mech has joined Rika's company to assist the four K1Rs Rika freed from the Politica in re-integration.

K1R mechs have a variety of heavy armament, including massive chainguns, railguns, missiles (with and without tactical nuke warheads), electron beams, and proton beams. They also sport a variety of suppression devices, from pulse, to sonic, to portable grav shields.

K1R mechs were not made later in the war, due to their cost and mental instability.

There were rumors that a limited run of K2R mechs were made, but no credible reports exist.

Sub-Models:

All K1R models could be outfitted with interchangeable armament, excepting the base model, which could not carry the tactical nukes.

K1R – The base K1R model was made in the early years of the war, and lacked the coordination and reactive armor of the later models.

K1R-M – The 'M' K1R added in the reactive armor, and included upgraded railguns with more advanced scan and target tracking systems. These mechs carried two missiles in launcher pods in their backs. They could be (and often were) upgraded to support the tactical nuke warheads on the missiles.

K1R-T – The 'T' model was a similar configuration to the 'M', but came standard with tactical nuclear warheads. Instead of the pair of launchers the K1R-M sported, the 'T' model carried as many as twelve missiles.

K1R-X-4 – 'M' and 'T' models both saw upgrades from Finaeus and the ISF engineers, which made them capable of functioning as AM or K1R models. None of the K1Rs opted to operate as AMs, but their 4th generation frames had considerable upgrades to power and armor. X-4 models have the ability to swap armament with AM models as well.

K2R-MBM – Based on designs Corporal Stripes stole at the end of the war, the K2R-MBM took the idea of a tank mech and raised the bar.

The Genevian military never had the energy to power their plans for the K2R mechs, but with miniaturized critical energy modules and ISF-grade SC batteries, the dreams of the GAF came into being under Finaeus's guidance.

The K2R-MBM is piloted by two AM-4 mechs (leveraging a part of the AM-T spec); one who manages movement and main-arm weapons, and another who controls the secondary arms, defensive systems, and secondary weapons systems.

On top of existing armament, the K2R-MBM brings to bear variable density proton beams, nanonet missiles, electron lashes, mortars (both thermite and HE), rapid-fire DPU cannons, as well as ground-hugger missiles.

The mech also functions as a re-armament center for its squad, and an attack drone deployment system.

AM (Assault Mech)

The AM mechs represented the bulk of the GAF's mechanized infantry program. It is estimated that over ten million AMs were created during the war, and over one hundred thousand are known to have survived. Many joined mercenary outfits or militaries of other nations.

AM model mechs were a 'torso-only' design, where none of the human's arms and legs were retained. The original idea was to make their cores swappable with K1R models, but it turned out that the mechanized infantry design of the AM models was generally more effective than the 'walking tank' design of the K1R models.

AM models were versatile mechs that had swappable loadouts. The improvements over time were mostly centered around human-mech integration, armor, and power systems.

AM mechs were often outfitted with chainguns, shoulder-mounted railguns, and electron beams.

Without known exception, AM mechs were always male.

Sub-Models

AM-1 – The original model of AM. Fewer than 100,000 AM-1 mechs were made, and none were known to have survived the war.

AM-2 – The AM-2 mechs quickly superseded the AM-1s, with better armor, more efficient power systems, and superior human-mech integrations.

AM-3 – The third generation of AM mech had upgraded power supply systems, and an artificial epidermis to remove the need for periodic removal and cleaning. Some AM-3s were also AI-capable.

AM-T – Design specs for AM-T mechs exist, but it is not known if any were made by the Genevians. The AM-T design utilized two AM-3 mechs working together in one larger body, controlling more limbs and separating motion and combat functions.

AM-4 – Designed by Finaeus Tomlinson, the AM-4 mechs are a step closer to humanity for the mechanized warriors. With stub limbs (like RR-3 and SMI models), the AM-4 mechs also utilize the MK99 chameleon armor epidermis.

AM-4s now support fully-swappable limbs with all other models, though they still possess the heaviest frames, and are capable of carrying heavier weapons, more ammunition, and heavier armor than any other mech type.

The 4th generation model now possesses internal, torso-mounted a-grav units for added mobility and stabilization.

RR (Recon/Ranger)

The RR model of mech was the precursor to the SMI model. RRs were based on both male and female humans, though smaller humans were used for RR models than AM and FR mechs.

These mechs were similar to AM models, except they were physically smaller and lighter. This allowed RRs to handle light aircraft/drop deployments.

As a compromise, they had smaller power sources, and could only operate for 2-3 days in the field.

Their loadouts were swappable with AM models, but they rarely utilized the chainguns.

Sub-Models

RR-1 – This model of mech began to appear on the battlefield around the same time as the AM-2 mechs. They utilized the power upgrade of the AM-2 mechs to have smaller power systems, but they also had a smaller power capacity. In theory, the new batteries of the AM-2 line should have worked, but they had overheating issues in the field, and more than one RR-1 had battery detonation when utilizing multiple firing systems.

RR-2 – The RR-2 mechs were rolled out around the same time as the AM-3s, and had few significant changes other than improved armor, and marginally longer-lasting power that no longer suffered from overload issues.

Second gen RR-2 mechs were also skinless, like AM-3 and SMI mechs.

RR-3 – The RR-3 mechs reached the field shortly before the end of the war, and were different in that they had partial legs, like SMI mechs. This was done as a cost/component-saving measure.

RR-4 – These mechs moved a step closer to the SMI spec, gaining the MK99 chameleon armor epidermis, and becoming lighter—even with their new stub limbs—thanks to advanced materials provided by the ISF.

The RR-4s use the same swappable weapons mounts as all mechs, but have high-output a-grav units in their thighs. These units allow them to fly at low altitudes (up to three hundred meters) and provide additional zero-*g* maneuvering options without using armor-based systems.

Seven of the RR-4s took the option for an additional set of arms and the brain modifications required to control the extra limbs.

FR (Force Recon)

Force Recon mechs were mechs that had the lighter drop capabilities of the RR mechs, with the additional power and armor of AM-3 models. All FR mechs were skinless.

Sub-Models

FR-1 – The first generation of FR mechs were limited run, and had both weight and power load distribution issues.

FR-2 – Second generation FR mechs solved many of the issues from the first generation, and were well regarded for their effectiveness.

XFR – The XFR model is not known to have been widely produced. This model had additional power and carrying capacity to utilize shoulder-mounted proton beams and chainguns. However, the mech's loadout made it almost as heavy as an AM-3 without the armor.

FR-4 – Though there is no FR-3 model, Finaeus and the members of Rika's Repair and Medical platoon decided to go with consistent generational numbering across all mechs.

The latest FR model gained the XFR's shoulder-mounted beam weapons: one an electron beam, and the other a high-output burst laser cannon. These weapons slot onto the wearer's back and slide up over the shoulder, where they are each capable of two-hundred-and-seventy-degree motion, even with the meter-long barrel on each.

Additional changes include a-grav stabilization similar to the AM-4s, and the same universal limb and weapons mounting system, as well as the MK99 chameleon epidermis.

SMI (Scout Mech-Integrated)

The final mech model produced at the end of the war was built out of a desire for a super-light mech that could be used in place of standard infantry in sniper/recon situations, and bring extreme fire to bear if desired.

SMI mechs were also cost-saving mechs, as they retained more of their human body components, making for fewer prosthetic neural connections. They also leveraged progress in muscle and bone augmentation that had been used in RR and FR mech models.

Mechs of this model were built exclusively from small, lithe women who could fit in the armor and still create a small profile.

Unlike other mech models, SMI mechs were never deployed with two functional hands. One was always a weapon mount.

SMI mechs are all skinless.

Sub-Models

SMI-1 – The first generation of SMI mechs had a short production run due to psychological issues. Because they retained more of their human bodies than other mechs, they ended up having additional dysphoria issues.

SMI-2 – Second generation SMI mechs had improved physical integrations and psychological conditioning that caused the mechs to view themselves as less human. However, in the field, it was observed to have the opposite effect, and SMI mechs retained a strong connection to their humanity.

SMI-3 – A few experimental SMI-3 models were produced near the end of the war. These models had more powerful legs and higher top speeds, and used a new short-barreled model of the GNR. Some SMI-3s were deployed with two GNRs and no 'regular' arm.

SMI-4 – Though there had always been rumors of an SMI-3, no one in the Marauders ever saw direct evidence that the model was produced. Still, for the same reasons as the FR-4s, the SMI range moved to '4' as well.

The SMI-4 mechs had few visible improvements to their configurations, excepting that they received the MK99 chameleon armor. Advanced materials shed over ten kilograms, while adding additional batteries and stronger bone and muscle enhancements. The SMI-4 armor also possesses the same chameleon capabilities as their skin.

While SMI-4s support the same universal weapons mount system as all mechs, they do not have the recoil control or power systems for some of the more powerful weapons, and stick to their tried and true rifles and GNRs.

LHO (Lateral Hyper Operation)

LHO mechs were a model created by Finaeus to suit the needs of shipboard operation in Rika's fleet. As the human crews within the 7th Marauder Fleet saw the skill and precision with which the ISF created the 4th Generation mechs, they began to request mechanization.

A problem the Marauder ships faced was that they were lightly crewed. To aid in solving this problem, Finaeus crafted a new mech body that was like an SMI in many respects, but possessed four arms and a slightly elongated torso. These mechs also had neural mods and brain alterations to handle operating a new set of limbs with full dexterity.

The desired—and achieved—result were mechanized humans capable of performing a taskload of two people. This ability created greater efficiency in the smaller crews, while also creating a formidable shipboard force to repel boarders if a ship were to come under attack while the bulk of its mechs were away on a mission.

The LHOs are all designated 4th Generation.

It should be noted that Finaeus had told Rika that 4-limbed mechs were not advisable due to the time it would take for their brains to learn how to manage the extra limbs.

This is why none of the LHO mechs have combat as a primary function, but are training for it. Some of the naval personnel who chose mechanization went for FR or SMI frames because they couldn't afford to take the time to learn how to manage extra limbs.

1st MARAUDER FLEET

This is a partial list and does not contain the full fleet roster.

Fleet Commander: Colonel Heather (SMI-4)

Fury Lance
4100-meter dreadnought
420 fighters
Ship's AI: Piper
Captain: Captain Heather (SMI-4)
Navigation: Chief Warrant Officer Garth
Weapons and Scan: Chief Warrant Officer Ona
(Note: Ona and Garth frequently switch roles)

Republic IV
1100-meter cruiser
44 fighters
Ship's AI: N/A
Captain: Lieutenant Travis (AM-4)

Undaunted
1130-meter cruiser
34 fighters
Ship's AI: N/A
Captain: Lieutenant Ferris
Chief Engineer: Chief Warrant Officer Lara

Asora
544-meter destroyer
Ship's AI: N/A
Captain: Lieutenant Klen (RR-4)
Weapons and Scan: Chief Ashley (LHO-4)

Chief Engineer: Chief Glen

Capital
612-meter destroyer
Ship's AI: N/A
Captain: Lieutenant Buggsie

Dropship Pilots
- Chief Warrant Officer (CWO-3) Charles 'Mad Dog'
- Chief Warrant Officer (CWO-2) Halley

THE QUEEN'S GUARD

Head of the Guard: Captain Chase (AM-4)

Guard Members

- Lieutenant Kelly (SMI-4)
- Corporal Keli (SMI-4)
- Corporal Shoshin (AM-4)

1st GENEVIAN MARAUDER BATTALION

In the shuffle where Rika became the Genevian Magnus, the Marauders were reorganized to have General Barne at the head of the military under the commander in Chief.

'HQ' COMPANY

Battalion Commander (CO): Colonel Silva (SMI-4)

'R' COMPANY (M&M)

Platoon Commander – Lieutenant "Bondo" Carson
- Corporal Stripes (AM-X)

Other company commanders
Captain Meagan – SMI-4 (O Company)
Captain Gytra – RR-4-F (R Company)
Captain Crispin – K1R-4-X (S Company)
Captain Penelope – RR-4-F (T Company)

'M' COMPANY

Note, not all personnel in the Company are listed.

Company HQ

Commanding Officer (CO): Captain Karen (FR-4)
First Sergeant: Tex (RR-4)
Gunnery Sergeant: Aaron (AM-4)

First Platoon

Platoon CO – First Lieutenant Chris (AM-4)
Platoon Sergeant – Staff Sergeant Kristian (RR-4-M)

First Squad
Sergeant Crunch (AM-4)
4 Fireteams (19 mechs)

FT 1-1
- CPL Ben (AM-4)
- PVT Al, 'Whispers' (AM-4)
- PVT Kim (RR-4-F)
- PVT Harris (FR-4)

FT 1-2
- CPL Kelly (SMI-4)
- PVT Shoshin (AM-4)
- PVT Keli (SMI-4)

FT 1-3
- CPL Kerry (RR-4)

FT 1-4

- CPL Mitch (RR-4)
- PVT Lauren (SMI-4)
- PVT Wolf (AM-4)
- PVT Matthew (AM-4)

Second Squad
Squad Sergeant – Corin (RF-4)
3 Fireteams (13 mechs)

FT 2-1
- CPL (K1R-X-4) Oosterwyk-Bruyn, 'The Van'
- PVT Ainsley (SMI-4)
- PVT Jenny (RR-4-F)

Third Squad
Squad Sergeant Carolyn 'CJ' (RR-4-F)
4 Fireteams (19 mechs)

FT 3-1
- PVT Kyle, 'Goob' (AM-4)
- CPL Yiaagaitia, 'Yig' (RR-4-M)
- PVT Cole (RR-4-F)
- PVT Fiona (SMI-4)

FT 3-2
- CPL Dave (AM-4)
- PVT Chad (FR-4)
- PVT Knight (AM-4)
- PVT Rouse (AM-4)

Fourth Squad
Squad Sergeant – Kara (SMI-4)
4 Fireteams (20 mechs)

Second Platoon

Platoon CO – First Lieutenant Fuller (AM-4)
Platoon Sergeant – Staff Sergeant Chauncy (FR-4)

Squad One
Squad Sergeant – Alison (SMI-4)
4 Fireteams (19 mechs)

FT 1-4
- CPL Fred (AM-4)
- PVT Jenisa (SMI-4)
- PVT Kor (AM-4)
- PVT Randy (AM-4)

Second Squad
Squad Sergeant – Tre (FR-4)
4 Fireteams (21 mechs)

Third Squad
Squad Sergeant Bean (SMI-4)
4 Fireteams (20 mechs)

FT 3-1
- CPL Hidee (SMI-4)

Fourth Squad
Squad Sergeant Kristina, 'Abs' (RR-4-F)
4 Fireteams (20 mechs)

FT 2-4
CPL Musel (AM-4)
PVT Bitty (K1R-X-4)
PVT Smitty (RR-4-F)

Third Platoon

Platoon CO – First Lieutenant Wilson (FR-4)
Platoon Sergeant – Staff Sergeant Bookie (SMI-4)

Squad One
Squad Sergeant Char (RR-4-F)
4 Fireteams (19 mechs)

Second Squad
Squad Sergeant Mal (FR-4)
4 Fireteams (22 mechs)

Third Squad
Squad Sergeant Cory (AM-4)
4 Fireteams (19 mechs)

Fourth Squad
Squad Sergeant Lana (SMI-4)
4 Fireteams (20 mechs)

'N' COMPANY

Note, not all personnel in the Company are listed.

Company HQ

Commanding Officer (CO): Captain Scarcliff (FR-4)
Executive Officer (XO): First Lieutenant Crudge (AM-4)
Gunnery Sergeant: Sergeant Johnny (FR-4)
Tactics and Strategy AI: Dredge

First Platoon

Platoon CO – First Lieutenant Michael (AM-4)
Platoon Sergeant – Staff Sergeant Alana (RR-4-F)

Squad One
Squad Sergeant Bruce (RR-4-M)
4 Fireteams (19 mechs)

Second Squad
Squad Sergeant Aerin (SMI-4)
4 Fireteams (21 mechs)

Third Squad
Squad Sergeant Justin (FR-4)
4 Fireteams (19 mechs)

Fourth Squad
Squad Sergeant Val (RR-4-F)
3 Fireteams (14 mechs)

Second Platoon

Platoon CO – Lieutenant Darla (RR-4-F)
Platoon Sergeant – Staff Sergeant Sal (FR-4)

Squad One
Squad Sergeant Sarah (RR-4-F)
4 Fireteams (19 mechs)

Second Squad
Squad Sergeant George (FR-4)
4 Fireteams (20 mechs)

Third Squad
Squad Sergeant Jessa (RR-4-F)
3 Fireteams (14 mechs)

Fourth Squad
Squad Sergeant Jynafer (RR-4-F)
3 Fireteams (13 mechs)

'Q' COMPANY

Note, not all personnel in the Company are listed.

Company HQ

Commanding Officer (CO): Captain Ron (AM-4)
Executive Officer (XO): First Lieutenant Bookie (SMI-4)

First Platoon

Platoon CO – First Lieutenant Layna (AM-4)
Platoon Sergeant – Staff Sergeant Boris (RR-4-F)

Squad One
Squad Sergeant Mela (RR-4-M)
4 Fireteams (19 mechs)

FT 1-1
Corporal Harlan (K1R-X-4)

THE BOOKS OF AEON 14

Keep up to date with what is releasing in Aeon 14 with the free Aeon 14 Reading Guide.

The Sentience Wars: Origins (Age of the Sentience Wars – w/James S. Aaron)
- Books 1-3 Omnibus: Lyssa's Rise
- Books 4-5 Omnibus (incl. Vesta Burning): Lyssa's Fire

- Book 0 Prequel: The Proteus Bridge (Full length novel)
- Book 1: Lyssa's Dream
- Book 2: Lyssa's Run
- Book 3: Lyssa's Flight
- Book 4: Lyssa's Call
- Book 5: Lyssa's Flame

The Sentience Wars: Solar War 1 (Age of the Sentience Wars – w/James S. Aaron)
- Book 0 Prequel: Vesta Burning (Full length novel)
- Book 1: Eve of Destruction
- Book 2: The Spreading Fire (Sept 2019)

Enfield Genesis (Age of the Sentience Wars – w/Lisa Richman)
- Book 1: Alpha Centauri
- Book 2: Proxima Centauri
- Book 3: Tau Ceti
- Book 4: Epsilon Eridani
- Book 5: Sirius

Origins of Destiny (The Age of Terra)
- Prequel: Storming the Norse Wind
- Prequel: Angel's Rise: The Huntress (available on Patreon)
- Book 1: Tanis Richards: Shore Leave
- Book 2: Tanis Richards: Masquerade
- Book 3: Tanis Richards: Blackest Night

- Book 4: Tanis Richards: Kill Shot

The Intrepid Saga (The Age of Terra)
- Book 1: Outsystem
- Book 2: A Path in the Darkness
- Book 3: Building Victoria

- The Intrepid Saga Omnibus – *Also contains Destiny Lost, book 1 of the Orion War series*

- Destiny Rising – *Special Author's Extended Edition comprised of both Outsystem and A Path in the Darkness with over 100 pages of new content.*

The Sol Dissolution (The Age of Terra)
- Book 1: Venusian Uprising (2019)
- Book 2: Scattered Disk (2020
- Book 3: Jovian Offensive (2020)
- Book 4: Fall of Terra (2020)

The Warlord (Before the Age of the Orion War)
- Books 1-3 Omnibus: The Warlord of Midditerra

- Book 1: The Woman Without a World
- Book 2: The Woman Who Seized an Empire
- Book 3: The Woman Who Lost Everything

The Orion War
- Books 1-3 Omnibus (includes Ignite the Stars anthology)

- Book 1: Destiny Lost
- Book 2: New Canaan
- Book 3: Orion Rising
- Book 4: The Scipio Alliance
- Book 5: Attack on Thebes
- Book 6: War on a Thousand Fronts
- Book 7: Precipice of Darkness
- Book 8: Airtha Ascendancy

- Book 9: The Orion Front
- Book 10: Starfire
- Book 11: Race Across Spacetime (2019)
- Book 12: Return to Sol (2019)

Building New Canaan (Age of the Orion War – w/J.J. Green)
- Book 1: Carthage
- Book 2: Tyre
- Book 3: Troy
- Book 4: Athens

Tales of the Orion War
- Book 1: Set the Galaxy on Fire
- Book 2: Ignite the Stars

Perilous Alliance (Age of the Orion War – w/Chris J. Pike)
- Book 1-3 Omnibus: Crisis in Silstrand

- Book 1: Close Proximity
- Book 2: Strike Vector
- Book 3: Collision Course
- Book 3.5: Decisive Action
- Book 4: Impact Imminent
- Book 5: Critical Inertia
- Book 6: Impulse Shock

The Delta Team (Age of the Orion War)
- Book 1: The Eden Job
- Book 2: The Disknee World (2019)
- Book 3: The Dark Twins (2020)

Rika's Marauders (Age of the Orion War)
- Book 1-3 Omnibus: Rika Activated

- Prequel: Rika Mechanized
- Book 1: Rika Outcast
- Book 2: Rika Redeemed
- Book 3: Rika Triumphant

- Book 4: Rika Commander
- Book 5: Rika Infiltrator
- Book 6: Rika Unleashed
- Book 7: Rika Conqueror

Non-Aeon 14 Anthologies containing Rika stories
- Bob's Bar Volume 2
- Backblast Area Clear

The Genevian Queen (Age of the Orion War)
- Book 1: Rika Rising
- Book 2: Rika Coronated
- Book 3: Rika Reigns (2019)

Perseus Gate (Age of the Orion War)
Season 1: Orion Space
- Episode 1: The Gate at the Grey Wolf Star
- Episode 2: The World at the Edge of Space
- Episode 3: The Dance on the Moons of Serenity
- Episode 4: The Last Bastion of Star City
- Episode 5: The Toll Road Between the Stars
- Episode 6: The Final Stroll on Perseus's Arm
- Eps 1-3 Omnibus: The Trail Through the Stars
- Eps 4-6 Omnibus: The Path Amongst the Clouds

Season 2: Inner Stars
- Episode 1: A Meeting of Bodies and Minds
- Episode 2: A Deception and a Promise Kept
- Episode 3: A Surreptitious Rescue of Friends and Foes
- Episode 4: A Victory and a Crushing Defeat
- Episode 5: A Trial and the Tribulations (2019)
- Episode 6: A Deal and a True Story Told (2019)
- Episode 7: A New Empire and An Old Ally (2019)
- Eps 1-3 Omnibus: A Siege and a Salvation from Enemies

Hand's Assassin (Age of the Orion War – w/T.G. Ayer)
- Book 1: Death Dealer
- Book 2: Death Mark (2019)

Machete System Bounty Hunter (Age of the Orion War – w/Zen DiPietro)
- Book 1: Hired Gun
- Book 2: Gunning for Trouble
- Book 3: With Guns Blazing

Fennington Station Murder Mysteries (Age of the Orion War)
- Book 1: Whole Latte Death (w/Chris J. Pike)
- Book 2: Cocoa Crush (w/Chris J. Pike)

The Empire (Age of the Orion War)
- Book 1: The Empress and the Ambassador
- Book 2: Consort of the Scorpion Empress (2019)
- Book 3: By the Empress's Command (2019)

ABOUT THE AUTHOR

Malorie Cooper likes to think of herself as a dreamer and a wanderer, yet her feet are firmly grounded in reality.

A twenty-year software development veteran, Malorie eventually climbed the ladder to the position of software architect and CTO, where she gained a wealth of experience managing complex systems and large groups of people.

Her experiences there translated well into the realm of science fiction, and when her novels took off, she was primed and ready to make the jump into a career as a full-time author.

A 'maker' from an early age, Malorie loves to craft things, from furniture, to cosplay costumes, to a well-spun tale, she can't help but to create new things every day.

A rare extrovert writer, she loves to hang out with readers, and people in general. If you meet her at a convention, she just might be rocking a catsuit, cosplaying one of her own characters, or maybe her latest favorite from Overwatch!

She shares her home with a brilliant young girl, her wonderful wife (who also writes), a cat that chirps at birds, a never-ending list of things she would like to build, and ideas...

Find out what's coming next at www.aeon14.com.
Follow her on Instagram at www.instagram.com/m.d.cooper.
Hang out with the fans on Facebook at
www.facebook.com/groups/aeon14fans.

Made in the USA
Columbia, SC
22 January 2021

31412707R00162